SWORD MOUNTAIN

SWORD MOUNTAIN

NANCY YI FAN

HARPER

An Imprint of HarperCollinsPublishers

Sword Mountain

Text copyright © 2012 by Nancy Yi Fan

Illustrations copyright © 2007 by Mark Zug

www.harpercollinschildrens.com

Library of Congress Cataloging-in-Publication Data

Fan, Nancy Yi.

Sword Mountain / Nancy Yi Fan. — 1st ed.

p. cm. — (Swordbird)

Summary: When adopted by the eagle prince, a valley-born eaglet must learn to become a princess and also a heroine.

ISBN 978-0-06-165108-3

1. Children's writings, American. [1. Birds—Fiction.
2. Adoption—Fiction. 3. Kings, queens, rulers, etc.—Fiction.
4. Heroes—Fiction. 5. Fantasy. 6. Children's writings.] I. Title.

PZ7.F19876Swk 2012   2011044621

[Fic]—dc23   CIP

                                                          AC

Typography by Amy Ryan

12 13 14 15 16   LP/RRDH   10 9 8 7 6 5 4 3 2 1

First Edition

TO ALL WHO HAVE WISHED
UPON A DANDELION

TABLE OF CONTENTS

PROLOGUE   *The Blank Letter*   xi

1. *A Light on the Mountain*   1

2. *The Castle of Sky*   11

3. *An Underground Affair*   21

4. *Uprooted*   31

5. *Pain in Painting*   45

6. *Between Mother and Son*   59

7. *Birds of a Feather*   73

8. *Aloft*   89

9. *Clash of Words*   99

10. *A Gap in the Iron Nest*   107

11. *Masquerade*   115

12. *The Flight Home*   125

13. *On the Making of a Tutor*   133

14. *A Legitimate Scandal*   143

15.   Owl Philosophies   155

16.   Packages of Trouble   175

17.   Tension   189

18.   The King's Birthday   195

19.   The Common Thread   205

20.   Within a Hundred Beats   217

21.   Out of Control   231

22.   Hurrying   245

23.   The Castle of Earth   255

24.   Consumed   267

25.   Funeral   281

26.   The Bronze Scales   287

27.   Excerpt from Songs and Records
      of Fleydur   301

EPILOGUE   Rising   305

MAJOR CHARACTERS   309

ACKNOWLEDGMENTS   313

*An ember that survives the rain burns to start
another flame.*
—FROM THE *BOOK OF HERESY*

PROLOGUE
THE BLANK LETTER

Kawaka tore open his emperor's last letter.

The war had been lost and Emperor Maldeor had been slain. Even the fire ants were attacking Kawaka as he lay on the battlefield. The archaeopteryx yearned for a message that would catapult him out of defeat and resurrect his empire.

Cryptic letters swirled on the parchment. Kawaka rubbed his eyes—no, there were only patterns of fire ants. He flicked the insects left and right, trying to see what they had obscured.

In the moonlight, the page shone blank.

Could that be Emperor Maldeor's entire legacy? He rattled the envelope again. Out fell another piece of paper, folded into a minuscule square. He held his breath as he smoothed the creases away. This time, he found directions to a cave.

The archaeopteryx's relief was cut off by the pain of an ant bite. "You think you have won?" he said to the ants as he tracked down the anthill. The thought of the eagles who'd led the opposing army made him demolish the mound with a kick.

Kawaka stuffed the blank page into a pocket and picked up the directions. For the next few hours he crossed a strait of the Kaurian Sea and continued inland. By dawn, he arrived before a cave.

Inside, he saw a book, a torch, and a glass vial on a stone pedestal against the back wall. He lit the torch and picked up the book. Three gold-inked words glinted at him from the leather cover: *Book of Heresy*. On the first page was a picture of the flag of the archaeopteryx empire billowing in the wind: khaki, saw edged, with an archaeopteryx's upheld wing emblazoned in the center. Below the illustration ran a bold script: "Archaeopteryxes are invincible—the empire forever lives on!"

The sight choked Kawaka with emotion. "Forever!" he cried. He clasped the book of his emperor, awed, for it contained wisdom gleaned from crushing a thousand enemies, fighting a thousand battles, and ruling the largest empire on the face of the world. Kawaka tucked the book carefully inside his uniform.

There was, however, still one item left. Kawaka grabbed the glass vial of liquid, opened it, and sniffed. Awful. His cry of disgust turned into a scream when a spilled drop splashed onto his foot. It was as if he had released invisible fire ants on himself. Kawaka yanked the blank sheet from his pocket and wiped frantically. He was about to crumple it up when he saw that where the liquid had touched the paper, words appeared.

Kawaka poured the rest of the liquid over it; soon a whole message rippled into view. "Not all is lost. Eradicate the golden eagles, and take their Sword Mountain to be our new capital. A map, weapons, and funds for this task are beneath the pedestal."

He heaved aside a panel of loose rock that hid a small passageway. Gold coins lined the floor; cutlasses hung from the walls. Kawaka armed himself and crammed the pockets of his uniform with gold.

Then Kawaka snatched the map. *Mere anthills*, he

thought as he glanced at the map's mountains. He bit a talon till it bled, and with blood drew a scarlet circle around the tallest summit on the mountain range. "My Sword Mountain," he whispered.

*The first taste of flight brings a sky of exhilaration
or an abyss of terror.*
—FROM THE OLD SCRIPTURE

1
A Light on the Mountain

Wind screeched across the Skythunder mountain range, wringing the rain clouds till every valley and every hill was glazed with rushing water. In the storm, lighting struck Sword Mountain, the tallest peak.

Crack! A bolt seared the soaring pillar of stone on the mountaintop.

"It's not just a piece of jutting rock," Fleydur, an

exiled eagle prince, used to explain when his minstrel wanderings took him to birds of the flatlands. "Sword Mountain controls the thoughts of birds who live on it. The mountain *is* law, reinforcing itself."

One part of that law was the caste system. In the daytime, it was very easy to see which eagles of Sword Mountain were of high rank and which were of low rank. The eagles in the valleys were peasants, herders who kept flocks of rodents. The artisans lived in the forested slopes above them; the elite, in mansions higher up. Above them all was a place reserved for the royal dead. Coffins of kings past were suspended upon the cliff side, as if to separate the other eagles from the king's castle on the very peak of the mountain.

But now each dwelling, whether high or low, was represented by a simple point of light, shimmering in the rain.

Tonight there was one light different from all others. It was a birthday candle.

In a small hut on the ledge of a cliff, Dandelion flapped newly fledged wings. Eagles considered the first day of having completely fledged wings a special sort of birth: They called it becoming sky-born. Today was Dandelion's sky-born day. Soon she would take her first flight.

"What does it take to fly?" the eaglet asked her mother.

"A fresh and steady wind," her mother replied. She peered anxiously through the rain. Her husband was hunting for a celebratory supper. Was the rain delaying him, or could it be his injuries? Some seasons ago, when the archaeopteryx empire had been at its peak of power, it had conquered new territories in the foothills of the Skythunder mountain range. After joining the Sword Mountain militia to defend the borders, the father eagle had lost all the talons on the toes of his left foot. Without those sharp curved nails, prey often wiggled and escaped.

"But once the wind is there, then what? What can I do to fly?" Hearing her eaglet's questions, the mother eagle tried to push aside her worries.

"Well," she said thoughtfully, "it does take a bit of reckless courage to throw yourself from a cliff, and it takes stubborn belief."

"But what will keep me up?"

"Why, that's something that has to come from the heart. It glows in you and propels you up just like a candle does in a sky lantern," the mother said. "To fly, you must have a special force inside you. Doubt is a heavy stone that will keep you on the ground. You can only fly when you use your force to clear your doubts away." The mother eagle nodded to herself, and then added, "But to fly well, you have to fall first."

Solemnly the eaglet looked into the flame of her birthday candle. Had she lived higher up the mountain, there would probably have been a grand cake in the shape of a pair of wings, but her mother was a weaver and her father a hunter. They could not afford such extravagance.

"Why does flight have to begin with a fall?" the eaglet whispered.

Her mother replied, "Doesn't everything in life start with a fall?"

It was at this moment that the father eagle returned. The mother greeted him with relief. "Here's some good news for you," the father said, beaming. "I heard from the innkeeper up the slope that Prince Forlath's army is returning. They've won! The archaeopteryx empire has been defeated. What a day. And look what I got for your birthday!" He lifted his claws for her and the eaglet to see his catch.

"A tortoise!" exclaimed the eaglet.

Her father had captured it and then flown high in the sky. He had dropped it down to crack it open, and now the shell was covered with fine cracks. "I thought I'd get something tasty," he said, patting the eaglet's head. "Something special for your birthday candle." He placed the tortoiseshell upon the stone table, and the mother eagle put the candle on top of the shell.

The little family admired the tortoise and the candle, the light dancing on their faces. "It's a proper cake!" said the eaglet. Her family laughed together.

"Remember, my child," her father said, "once you blow out the candle, you will not be a hatchling anymore, but a true eagle, as brave as the eagles who fought with Prince Forlath. Eagles don't pull back from a rough wind, but always dare to ride on it—"

The candle flame abruptly slanted. The eaglet held her breath while her father turned at the sound of somebird landing outside their cave. "Who's there?" he called.

They only heard scraping sounds of claws on stone. Then a cough.

The eaglet's smile faded. She looked to her mother for guidance and was tucked beneath her mother's wing. All three saw the profile of a gaunt reptilelike bird appear in the entrance. And the flash of a cutlass. "Food," a harsh voice commanded. "Give me food."

It was a rain-splattered archaeopteryx, drawn by the firelight and seeking shelter.

He stepped into the hut.

"Kawa," the father eagle said under his breath, recognizing the distinct beak of the archaeopteryx empire's head knight. He exchanged glances with his wife. How had this dangerous bird slipped through the lines of the eagle army to Sword Mountain?

Dandelion's father did not look down at her birthday tortoise, but beyond, at the empty cupboards and shelves. The archaeopteryx pointed at the tortoise. "What's that." It wasn't a question, but a command.

Reluctantly the father picked up the tortoise, and still more reluctantly, he offered it to him. With a snort, Kawaka knocked aside the candle on the shell, and the eaglet watched the flame die, and shut her eyes. She heard the archaeopteryx sniff the meat, taste it, and finally devour it in several huge bites. "More," Kawaka growled.

"We have nothing else," said the mother.

The archaeopteryx leaned forward. "You refuse my orders?" His claws tightened on the hilt of his cutlass, but then his eyes fell upon the eaglet, and his expression changed.

The eaglet opened her eyes and saw that the archaeopteryx's beak was disfigured, curved to one side, demonically clownish. His breath stank of carrion. He lifted a gnarled foot and walked forward a few steps. The eaglet edged back. "What a sweet little bird," he cackled, his eyes fastened on Dandelion.

"Don't you dare lay a talon upon my hatchling!" the mother yelled.

"I do what I wish," snarled Kawaka. He leaped toward the eaglet, but her mother scrambled forward and was immediately upon him. The force of her attack sent the cutlass out of his claws and knocked both of them over the ledge and into the air below. Despite her mother's anger and size, the archaeopteryx had much more experience with fighting.

"Stay here! Be careful!" her father told Dandelion as he whipped past. He dived repeatedly at the archaeopteryx, raking him with his only talons. From the rock ledge, Dandelion watched, shivering, holding on to her extinguished birthday candle.

"I don't need two of you at once!" she heard the archaeopteryx cry. Kawaka yanked something from his belt and twisted around to face the female eagle. Then he detached himself from her talons and swooped up. But the mother eagle continued to fall, her great wings flapping in the wind like rags. She knocked against the cliff and rolled down a few feet before she disappeared from the eaglet's sight on the forest floor.

"Mama!" Panic seized the eaglet. She dashed to the edge of the cave, trying to peer below. Her mother was slumped on the ground, almost as if she were brooding eggs. Dandelion forgot everything but one thought: *How?* How to reach her mother? Her claws scrabbled on the stone beneath her. She could not climb down the sheer cliff. Then, in a sudden burst, Dandelion leaned forward, beat her wings, and jumped.

First flight.

No, it was a first fall, and an intentional fall. Dandelion didn't want to rise up to the sky. She didn't try to flap her wings. Wind pressed by her ears, cold and full of rain, but she was too numb to feel afraid. She still clutched her candle, clinging to the warmth that had been there only moments ago. Trees below the cliff hurtled into her vision. In the corner of her eye her father roared with pain and fury as he fought with the archaeopteryx, but Dandelion could not forget her mother.

"Please get up, Mama," she cheeped feebly as the ground rushed up at her.

Then all was darkness.

*When the wind blows a dandelion seed to a strange
land, will it thrive?*
—FROM THE OLD SCRIPTURE

2
THE CASTLE OF SKY

Amid the jingling of bells, Fleydur the bard knelt and cupped his talons around the little bird's face.

"She will come home with us," he said.

Prince Forlath uncovered the broken hilt of a cutlass from pine needles. The troops behind them grew quiet, and all watched as Fleydur wrapped the eaglet into a blanket.

"Fleydur," murmured Forlath to his older brother. "You know you shouldn't."

"Shouldn't take care of a little injured one like this?" said Fleydur.

Forlath turned aside, but an eagle warrior behind Fleydur said, "She doesn't belong on the mountaintop." The troops mumbled in agreement.

"You know the customs. . . ."

"There is no room for outsiders, not up there!"

"Fleydur, it'll be too risky for you," said Forlath at last. "Bringing a valley bird to the castle will not help your cause."

"My freedom. My life. Aren't those all I have to lose? I'm making the choice to come back home, and to face any risks I might find there," said Fleydur. "This eaglet did not choose to suffer like this. I—we—have to help her now."

Fleydur had not placed a talon in his birthplace for twenty seasons, but he felt that Sword Mountain had been suspended in time. As he led the procession into the audience chamber, he noticed in disbelief that the advisers of the court still stood in the same positions. Their faces, surrounded by a golden swirl of dust motes, bore fossilized expressions.

"You—" King Morgan stood up sharply and hobbled toward them.

The guards flanking the throne all stiffened, their eyes fastened on Fleydur, everybird recalling the last words Morgan had shouted at his minstrel son. *"Do you care so much for others, and place them before your own tribe? It's beneath you. Go, then. Go to your starving friends and throw your dignity to the winds. You are not my son anymore!"* Tension rose in the air, bordering on hostility.

Forlath looked at Morgan. "Father, surely—"

Morgan paid no attention. He rushed to Fleydur, his voice hoarse as he cried, "I expelled you from Sword Mountain. I had your name forbidden. I warned you that I never wanted to see you again, and you had the nerve to come back! This is your punishment—"

Fleydur shut his eyes.

"—come and give your father a hug." Tears rolled down his cheeks as he extended both wings to Fleydur.

The tension shattered as the birds all around burst into applause.

Morgan reached up a claw to touch Fleydur's face. "I almost cannot believe it . . . is it really true?" He turned to his younger son, Forlath. "I'm so thankful that you have found and brought to me . . . my Fleydur." The patriarch blinked waveringly. "Forgive me, Fleydur.

The strains of keeping our kingdom out of the claws of archaeopteryxes made me overreact when I saw you stray from our traditions. I have realized I was desperately trying to maintain order."

"And there shall be order, Father; worry no more," Fleydur said. "Forlath and I have helped win the archaeopteryx war."

Morgan snapped his claws for the attendants to bring over a wooden chest. "Fleydur, Fleydur. How you've changed. What travels you've been on! But now your journey's ended—you'll stay, surely you'll stay with your father now." Morgan swallowed. "Won't you?" Abruptly he busied himself, opening the chest and pulling something out.

"I've come home so that I—" Fleydur started to say.

"Oh, Fleydur," the king interrupted with a short laugh. "You know that whatever you may be, foremost, you still are a prince. By birth, by training"—he leaned forward and gently placed a gold circlet on Fleydur's head—"and by responsibility." Morgan happily adjusted a red velvet cloak around his son's shoulders. "What can I say?" murmured Morgan. "Doesn't he look fine?"

Queen Sigrid stood up. "Surely, Morgan, you jest."

Unlike the king, who had withered since Fleydur's departure, she had grown taller, plumper, and fuller of life. "Fleydur should either wear the clothes of the prince or those of a musician. They don't go together. Red velvet with those loud stripes and polka dots. Ridiculous!" she cackled, fanning herself. "And in my frank opinion, Fleydur seems more suited to the latter."

Sigrid threw a glance at Forlath. "You will support this, won't you, my dear son? Welcome back, Forlath. You were most sorely missed." She paused long enough for all birds' smiles to fade except her own.

"Well, Fleydur?" Sigrid turned back to him. "You may change clothes as you see fit after the formalities," she said, squinting. "But I believe I really must ask you to not break your father's heart again."

"I will not," Fleydur promised.

Morgan coughed. "How could he? The archaeopteryxes are defeated; our troubles are cast aside. To celebrate Fleydur's return, I will allow music."

As he got the difficult, painful word out, tranquillity softened his features. "Ah, both my sons. Together at my side in the last few moons of my old age. Nothing is more important than keeping a family together."

Fleydur raised his head at the word, for it was like a cue. "Father," he said.

"Yes, my son?"

"What about a bird who has lost her family? Would you let me take in an orphan, Father?"

"What's this?" Sigrid's smile sagged into a frown.

Fleydur turned back. Two warriors edged forward, a sling between them. Gesturing at the small inert figure in the sling, Fleydur said, "We came across this eaglet below our mountain, unconscious. There has been an archaeopteryx attack."

The birds of the court gaped as Forlath produced the broken cutlass for them to see. "A lone attacker. We've defeated the main army, but stragglers could cause trouble," he said.

"No relatives, no neighbors? You bring *it* here?" Sigrid asked.

"None that we found." Fleydur stroked the eaglet with a wing tip. "See, she's just an eaglet, and badly wounded. She probably spent all last night in the rain, and that didn't help."

"Take in a valley bird?" muttered Sigrid to herself. Surely every well-bred summit bird knew the rule of the mountain. *Fleydur's become worse than bold,* she thought.

She glared at Fleydur, then at the waif wrapped in a blanket beside him. Only the eaglet's head was visible.

Dirt freckled her face. Sigrid shuddered and rubbed her own claws, brushing away imaginary mud.

"Naturally it's suffering. Think of the hygiene of those eagles living down in the valley!" Sigrid attempted to look considerate. She then gestured to an attendant. "Put her in the dungeon. There's plenty of room there, if memory serves me correctly. She can have a ladleful of gruel."

"But why not house her in the guest wing? She's done nothing wrong to deserve the dungeon. And she can't possibly survive there." Fleydur's eyes flickered toward his father.

The king nodded. To the queen's chagrin, he agreed to Fleydur's request. "Of course my physician will treat her. She can remain until she is well."

Sigrid sucked in her breath, looking as if she would pinch or slap somebird. Such an insignificant eaglet, enjoying such privileges! She shot a glance at her son Forlath. Forlath appeared neutral. She turned to her favorite advisers. They stood glowering, as if a bucket of rank mud had just been emptied over their heads, but they didn't dare contradict the king.

The veins on Sigrid's neck strained. Why had Fleydur staged such a show, saving a valley eaglet? What further breaches of their traditions would he attempt? The king, much too old and much too unquestioning, did not see the risks his wayward son presented. It would fall to Sigrid to make sure that Fleydur and his unconventional love of music could do no harm to the mountain.

You never know who will knock at your door.
—FROM THE *BOOK OF HERESY*

3
AN UNDERGROUND AFFAIR

W hen night fell upon the mountain, the sky began raining ink.

"These eagles in their homeland are fiercer than those who've fought overseas!" Kawaka the archaeopteryx cried to himself, shuddering, too tired and too wet to fly. He'd had a hard time fighting with the eagle parents and had lost one of his cutlasses, but he had shown those two eagles who was stronger.

As Kawaka trudged through the Sword Mountain valley, holding a rhubarb leaf as an umbrella, his zeal to lay siege to the eagle stronghold began to ooze out of him like the blood out of his wounds.

"What can a single wounded archaeopteryx do to a fortified kingdom?" He paused as he glimpsed a ledge of rock in front of him, next to the curtain of a small waterfall. He ducked under the shelter. It was too dark for him to see beyond his beak, and even if he could, the rain had blurred his map. Nonetheless, Kawaka went through the motions of unrolling the map and of pushing it up close to his eyes. In despair, he cried out, "Nothing. I am lost."

He smelled the scent of earth coming from some-place behind the waterfall. *Well, I can't get any wetter now,* he thought, and clambered through the spray. There was a warm cave on the other side. He walked even deeper.

"If I had a battalion, I might weaken the eagles. But no allies . . . no knowledge of the enemy, either." Kawaka groaned. "I have nowhere to go. I am going nowhere."

He was wrong: Suddenly his beak banged into an iron door.

The door creaked open. Two glowing orange eyes stared out of the darkness; the eyes widened. There was a small torch inside the door, and its light illuminated a rusty nameplate:

TRANGLARHAD
The High Owl of Optical Theories (H.O.O.T.)
Alchemist, Owner, and Manager of the Knautyorsbut
Mine
Transactions Welcome

But as Kawaka opened his beak to speak, the door slammed shut in his face. From the other side, Tranglarhad's doorkeeper abandoned his post and hurled himself through the underground caverns, screeching, "Horrors! An archaeopteryx knocking at our door!" Hearing the echo of his voice, owl miners abandoned their work to cluster together and mutter anxiously.

In the very center of the maze of caverns was a huge laboratory with its own furnace. Tranglarhad, the High Owl, was hunched before the fire, furiously grinding a dark piece of glass into the shape of a lens. He was a slight-framed eagle owl with short legs but a neck stretched from always trying to peer around corners. He was in his usual attire: sunglasses, bow tie, tailed coat, and a studded belt with two square cleavers buckled one on each side.

"High Owl, come! There's an archaeopteryx!"

At the moment the doorkeeper appeared, Tranglarhad was raising the polished lens to compare it to another one.

"What?" Tranglarhad sputtered, and the glass lenses fell out of his claws and cracked on the ground. "Ah, glass ruined. And now, a murderer up and about." He snatched off his glasses, thrust them in the breast pocket of his coat, and quickly followed his doorkeeper.

"Why, I say! What are you here for?" The owl opened the iron door. "Your emperor sent you here to claim my mine, did he not, bird?" A square cleaver gleamed as he snatched it from his belt.

"No. I'm by myself. The archaeopteryx empire is no more. Let me in. I only want a place to rest and heal for a couple of weeks," Kawaka mumbled. Inwardly, he was much alarmed by meeting this new enemy. "Look, I'm unarmed. And wounded badly. I won't hurt you." *For now, at least.*

"But why choose to stay at *my* underground castle?" Tranglarhad objected, tightening his grip on the cleaver. "You realize the eagles' homes are just upstairs? I, ah, advise you to remove yourself."

Kawaka gritted his teeth. He needed an ally. The owl might have some information that he'd need about the eagles. As a last resort, he reached inside his uniform and tossed a glinting gold coin.

Tranglarhad's eyes lit up. "Oh no no no, stay, stay! Welcome!" The coin rose in an arc and fell clinking onto the stone floor.

The owl raised a foot and abruptly stepped on the coin. He picked it up and bit the edge to check if it was real gold. "Ah, the taste of money. Lovely." His demeanor swiftly changed. "A place to stay, you say? Now that I think of it, there is some room with us, oh, yes. One of my subjects will see to your cuts—ah, a friend in need is a friend indeed." He swept open the door and bowed, putting his cleaver back into his belt and dropping the coin into his pocket in one swift motion. "Tranglarhad, at your service."

Kawaka staggered inside, his sigh of relief cut off when he saw that Tranglarhad was the only owl who was smiling. He felt a tinge of apprehension as the iron door sealed shut behind him, but he reassured himself that he would be able to control the owls once he healed.

Led to the laboratory, Kawaka sat near the furnace. Tranglarhad provided him his dinner: a bucket of raw earthworms with a pepper shaker and a fork. "What do you think is especially unusual or important about Sword Mountain?" Kawaka asked, slurping the worms as if he were eating spaghetti. Why had Maldeor chosen Sword Mountain as the place to rebuild the archaeopteryx empire?

"Me and my associates!" Tranglarhad the owl ruffled his feathers majestically. "We've claimed an excellent vein of iron ore, whatever eagles think about owning everything on the mountain. Most birds don't know of my Castle of Earth. Who'd guess somebird would 'undermine' the eagles?" Tranglarhad's chuckling hoot bounced in the caverns.

"No." Kawaka gulped down an earthworm with impatience. "I mean, is there anything particular about the *eagles*?"

Tranglarhad waved his talons as if dismissing a fly. "Yes, yes, the golden eagles rule upstairs in their petty Castle of Sky. But what are they? I have either everything they have, or better. They have brawn? I have brain. Say that they have sharp eagle eyes? My night vision and sharp hearing rival that! Golden eagles? Why, holy hoot," Tranglarhad cried. "I am an *eagle* owl!"

Kawaka considered for a moment. "Then if you were to face them in battle, would you reach a stalemate?"

"Battle?" Tranglarhad indignantly spat an owl pellet. "Not for the likes of me. All that raucous noise, spewed guts, and whatnot . . . just about eliminates any art from the craft of . . . shall we say? Deflating the enemy."

"And how would you deflate them?" Kawaka asked.

"With knowledge," said Tranglarhad. "The golden eagles' downfall shall stem from their pride. So proud, some of them, on their rock tip, they can't see past their beaks. All they think of is traditions, position, and status. You won't see a valley eagle on the mountaintop. They don't mix. These very divisions make them suspicious, blind, weak."

Kawaka grunted, impressed.

"But you never know," Tranglarhad cautioned. "While Morgan the eagle king is aging into a doddering dotard, either of his sons has enough influence to change things, now they've returned victorious, I hear." Tranglarhad fanned his ear tufts apologetically at Kawaka.

"Don't be sorry. The archaeopteryxes won't remain pitiful," Kawaka growled, smoothing the remnants of his uniform.

What luck! he thought. If he had this peculiar personage working for him, it would be possible to establish a new archaeopteryx capital on Sword Mountain and spread the *Book of Heresy*. All Kawaka needed was to convince the owl to bring down the Skythunder eagles by employing his trickery. *And if he gets caught and perishes, I will not be harmed,* thought Kawaka.

Tranglarhad blinked his round eyes. Kawaka seemed so pensive, he couldn't help feeling suspicious. "But what really brings *you* to Sword Mountain?" he asked.

"Vengeance!" Kawaka snapped. "If it hadn't been for the golden eagles, we could have come to the rescue of our emperor." Kawaka pointed a wing at Tranglarhad. "I need you. A creature of night like you." Kawaka drew out the *Book of Heresy* from within his uniform and opened to a page. "See, this is what my emperor wrote. 'Darkness is power, because darkness is intimate. The haunting of a nightmare can hurt worse than the wound from a sword.'"

Now it was Tranglarhad's turn to be gleeful. *Holy hoot, such a valuable tool, this archaeopteryx,* he thought. *All blind emotion and no intellect. And his book, too, looks intriguing indeed.* "Well, I don't know," drawled the owl.

"Oh, did I mention—I have more money?" said Kawaka. He threw Tranglarhad a second gold coin.

"Your cause seems worthy," Tranglarhad said slowly, pocketing the coin. "And it kindles in me a desire to see the downfall of the eagles, after all. Certainly they've been bothering me lately, poking about my mine. And I want a certain item in their possession. Yes, it occurs to me that we should perhaps become allies," said the owl, offering a set of thick, fuzzy talons.

Kawaka extended his clammy foot and shook the owl's claws. "It is agreed."

There was a pause as each villain silently congratulated himself.

Then Kawaka sighed deeply. "It won't be a problem for me to get some of my former soldiers to come here once I'm better. But tell me—what do the eagles have that you want?"

"I recently heard tales of a precious dark crystal in their castle." Tranglarhad watched for Kawaka's reaction.

"A Leasorn gem!" Kawaka gasped.

"I have a special use for this stone, but that is for later. What concerns you and me the most—removing the stone would be an apt first step to weaken the eagles, would it not?"

"True," Kawaka allowed. "How and when do you think it will be possible?"

"I am confident the opportunity will present itself by and by," replied the owl, turning his face upward in the direction of the summit. He thrust on his dark glasses. "And when the opportunity comes, upon my pellet, I shall see it."

*If a bird lower than yourself has an advantage you
cannot have, O worry not, worry not! What can
you do to reassure yourself of your superiority?
Scorn, slander, and slam the door.*
—FROM THE *BOOK OF HERESY*

4
UPROOTED

Thousands of miles aboveground, the valley eaglet who had aroused the disapproval of the queen, the generosity of the king, and the compassion of the princes slowly opened her eyes. Remnants of nightmares fled from her, but she remembered nothing. Nothing, save for one sharp image—an archaeopteryx swiping stained claws at her. *"Fly, little eagle! Where will you go?"*

She didn't want to think of the archaeopteryx. Taking a deep breath, she looked around her. She was in a huge bed. Some golden eagles whom she'd never seen before loomed over her.

"She's awake!" Fleydur announced.

"Mama? Papa? Where is my candle?" Feverishly, her gaze drifted from the bandages on her wings to the faces around her.

Fleydur and Forlath exchanged glances. It was Forlath who finally spoke. "We're still searching for your parents, young one, but you're holding your candle."

The eaglet looked down, and indeed the candle was there in her clenched claws: barely melted, speckled with globules of wax. A smile flitted across her face. Fleydur, watching, felt his heart wrench. "What's your name?"

"Dandelion."

"I'm Fleydur; this is my brother, Forlath. You were injured when we found you, so we've brought you here to heal. You'll be all right, Dandelion. We'll make sure you're all right." Fleydur turned to the physician besides him, who nodded in agreement.

"Thank you," said the eaglet. She looked at her candle again. "I want to go home. When will I see my mother and father?"

"We'll find them as soon as we can," said Forlath.

"I miss them." Her eyes moistened. "They worked so hard so I could have a special, beautiful candle for my sky-born day."

"Can you give me your candle to hold, so I can take a look at your talons?" asked the physician. "You've been clutching it tightly even though your talons are bleeding."

Hesitantly, Dandelion held out the candle. "Can you put it by my pillow, please?" she said, and when the physician obliged, she laid her cheek against the candle. "It's my birthday candle. My mother and father were going to sing 'Happy Birthday' to me," she said.

"I can sing it now," said Fleydur. "Would you like me to sing it now?"

Dandelion nodded.

"Happy birthday to you . . . ," sang Fleydur.

Weak from her wounds, Dandelion gradually fell back into a merciful sleep.

Dandelion was alone when she awoke again, her broken wings encased in bandages but her mind clearer than before.

Where am I? she wondered. *I don't remember Fleydur and Forlath telling me. This place feels too airy for the valley.* Dandelion turned her face to the evening light from the window.

A wide blue sky stretched out before her eyes, with ragged gray points below. Mountaintops. *But the clouds are all wrong,* she thought. They were below her! She was looking at them from above.

Which meant Dandelion was higher than she had ever been, ever imagined. The tallest place she knew was the home of the eagle king, on top of Sword Mountain, but—how impossible. How ridiculous! How . . . ?

She slumped back into the silk covers of her bed, heart pounding. Gulping in lungfuls of perfumed air, she didn't have to look hard to find evidence of wealth: Gilded mirrors, marble busts of birds, and a domed ceiling painted blue filled her vision. The handles on the drawers were made of silver. The doorknob was crystal.

Before she could try to make sense of this, the doorknob on the thick oak door turned, and a female golden eagle not much older than herself stepped in.

Is she a princess? Dandelion thought. She did dress fancily enough, with a frilly cap framing her face and ribbons tied into bows on each of her ankles. A golden brooch shaped like half of an acorn adorned her collar.

As if sensing Dandelion's confusion, she flicked her ribboned feet. "I am Lady Olga to you. My great-great-great-grandfather was a member of the court. I have seen both the king and the queen, and I get to eat caviar."

Dandelion looked at the caviar eater, and Olga looked back, expecting her to be awed.

"This is the Castle of Sky, if you don't know. The grandest place in the Skythunder mountain range," Olga went on. "The princes Fleydur and Forlath brought you here."

"They're princes!" exclaimed Dandelion.

Olga sniffed. "Well, it was all very unusual, but I suppose it was a merely a gesture to celebrate their victory in the war. They wanted you to be like a regular visiting eaglet, so you were assigned a companion to keep you company and bring you meals. Unfortunately that was me." Olga allowed a condescending smile. "Consider yourself lucky to even step one talon here. I bet you've never taken classes with a tutor of the castle. I bet you don't know how to hold a teacup properly. I bet you don't even know what caviar is."

"I can learn," Dandelion said.

Olga snorted.

"There must be something I can do here once I'm better," said Dandelion, "to repay the princes who've saved me before I go home again."

The word home was a trigger, and tears leaked from Dandelion's eyes no matter how hard she squinted. Olga stared at her. "You mean you *want* to go home?" she said, surprised. "You'd rather be home than here?" She waved a wing tip at the luxurious room.

Dandelion nodded. She knew there was only one method of getting off this precipice: flight. She wanted to fly, so suddenly and so much it surprised her. If her wings weren't broken, if she knew how to fly, she could return to her home at once.

Yet there was a fear, a fear of . . . of . . . she was afraid of flying. Or was it of falling?

"I suppose everybird likes home best, even if yours is in the valley," Olga said slowly. "You certainly don't have to stay here. If you stay, they're just going to make a fool of you." Olga leaned in. "A *valley* fool. You're in luck, though, because I can take you back down."

Olga walked over to the window and slid it open. At once a fresh, glorious breeze sprang in, billowing the tasseled curtains, snapping the corners of the embroidered bedspread, and stirring the few uncovered feathers on Dandelion's wings.

Dandelion looked at her bandaged, broken wings. "Take me home," she said. She looked out the window. The sky was a vivid royal blue, and stars were emerging.

Dandelion was lying inside a gigantic wicker laundry basket, secured in the folds of sheets, her candle tucked by her side. "Olga?"

"Be quiet, will you?" said Olga. She and another eaglet, who also wore half a gold acorn pin, held the handles of the basket as they flew out of the castle courtyard.

"Olga, just one thing, please!"

"We're not turning back." Olga's voice turned malicious.

"No. Can you fly a little higher? I want to have a look."

There was a pause, and then Dandelion felt the basket starting to rise. Below, she could see the dark smudges of the forest and the castle, too. How beautiful it was, with majestic stained-glass windows that showed silhouettes of birds moving behind them. In a level field lower down the mountain, she saw eaglets playing lacrosse under the lantern light.

"She's so heavy!" shouted the other eaglet to Olga. "Come on, let's put her down on a ledge and rest a moment."

They chose the top of a small slope. Dandelion saw that Olga looked unhappy and frightened. She handed Dandelion a crust of bread and a flagon of something warm. Soup. "Eat," she said. The other eaglet whispered something in Olga's ear and slipped away. Dandelion gripped the warm bottle of soup, a sickening feeling dawning upon her. She choked down the soup and didn't have to wait long for what she feared would happen.

"Wait here," Olga muttered, her eyes elsewhere. "That eaglet, she has cold talons. She doesn't want to fly down in the dark. I'll be back soon, I'll get somebird else to carry you with me." She smoothed her frilly cap and lumbered off into the night, and Dandelion heard the sound of her rustling ankle ribbons fade.

Has she abandoned me? Dandelion wondered. Somehow it didn't seem unlikely. With her wings bound to awkward splints, she could not get anywhere by herself, so she would just have to wait for Olga to come back.

Dandelion craned her neck to look around. Uphill, she could glimpse the lights from the castle. Below was a steep outcropping, and she could make out the abodes of well-to-do eagles. All were out of shouting distance.

Sighing, Dandelion leaned back in the basket and watched the stars. A gust of wind picked up in the mountain, and Dandelion held her candle tighter, wondering whether anybird would find her. *I wish I was with Mama and Papa.*

Suddenly the stars lurched in her vision. She realized that that her basket was moving, sliding ever so slightly on the slope's loose rocks. Dandelion's first impulse was to get out, but when she sat up, the splint of one wing jammed into a gap in the weave of the basket, sending the basket careening.

"Ah—!" Rolling on a bed of pebbles, the basket picked up speed, and Dandelion could only grip the edges in terror. She was indeed heading for a drop-off.

She heard shouts of alarm from some eagles who appeared below her on the slope, but as they hollered, she zipped passed them. They pumped their wings to chase after her speeding basket. A golden blur pulled ahead of the group.

Whack.

Something stopped her basket abruptly. Dandelion looked over her shoulder. A lacrosse stick was hooked onto one of the handles.

"Nice catch, captain," some eaglet said in admiration. "Best save ever."

Talons pulled the basket to a flatter patch of ground. The lacrosse players gathered around Dandelion. The owner of the lacrosse stick was an eagle whose plumage was not the usual brown, but so light that it was tawny.

He and the other birds gawked at Dandelion. She

realized that with her bandages she resembled a mummy in a casket, but when the eaglet with the lacrosse stick laughed, it was a friendly sound.

"Great Spirit, some fight you must have been in to get that look. To think you almost broke more bones," he said to Dandelion, flashing a grin. "I'm Cloud-wing."

"Thanks for saving me," said Dandelion, smiling weakly. "I need to go home." *To the valley.*

"Definitely," another eaglet spoke. "We can give you a lift. What quarter do you live in?" He pointed his beak at the mansions in the distant cliffs.

Could they possibly think I'm one of their own? Dandelion thought. "I'm not a noble," she said. "I didn't mean to come up here."

Silence.

"A valley bird!" one of Cloud-wing's teammates cried out. All the eaglets except Cloud-wing suddenly backed off. They sneaked looks at one another, beaks hanging open.

"How did she get up here?" one muttered.

Cloud-wing turned to look at that bird. "What does that matter?"

Then there was a fluttering of wings. Olga landed on the cliff, followed by another eaglet.

"Sorry for the wait," she said to Dandelion breathlessly.

She turned to the eaglet she'd brought. "Come on, let's go."

The lacrosse team stepped back, unsure of what was happening.

"Olga!" exclaimed Cloud-wing. "You know this eaglet?"

"Oh, hello there." Olga smoothed the ribbon on one foot with the toes of the other. "She's Fleydur's eaglet. I was assigned to be her companion." Striding over, she gripped a handle of the basket. Her friend lifted the other one.

"Then you're supposed to make her feel welcome," said Cloud-wing. "Why did you take her outside?"

Olga braced herself to fly. "She's homesick," she explained. But just as Olga was about to leap into the air, Cloud-wing raised his lacrosse stick and barred the way.

"You can't do this," he said to them.

"Why not?" said Olga, taken aback. "I'm trying to help, is all!"

"You left her stuck in that basket on the slope, don't you know? The basket almost slid off the edge. That was dangerous! You don't know what you're doing. You don't even know where her home is, and her injuries are not healed," Cloud-wing cried. "She can't survive on her own like this."

On her own.

His last sentence struck an unknown dread in Dandelion. On her own? But she was going home to her mother and father, wasn't she?

Again she had the brief image of the archaeopteryx slashing at her in her mind, but now the image progressed, and she remembered a little more, a few seconds more, of her mother . . . frantically her mind started shutting off. She could not think. She could not feel. She could not move. Her throat clenched, pinching off her air passage.

"What's wrong with her?" yelled Olga, dropping the basket on the ground. The eaglets crowded around, frightened and worried. More birds were coming toward them now. Older eagles joined their ranks.

Dandelion heard jabbering voices dimly, but she could not respond. She didn't want to see. She didn't want to know. Most of all, she didn't want to remember. She was blissfully frozen, and shadows pooled in her vision.

When Dandelion's mind recovered, she was exhausted and weak and tucked into the bed of her sickroom. It was late at night. Candles cast a soft, mellow glow all around her.

The door creaked, and Olga stood in the doorway, unsmiling.

"I didn't mean for any of this to happen," said Dandelion, but Olga did not listen.

"I was just trying to help," Olga cried. "Now I'm in trouble with everybird, including the princes. And it's your fault. See if I ever offer to do you a favor again. You even made me look bad in front of—" She shut her beak on the words and scowled at Dandelion. "Humph! All pitiful in bandages, so they feel sorry for you. But underneath"—Olga jabbed a claw at Dandelion's acorn-less collar—"you're still a *valley* bird." She spun around and stormed away, slamming the door shut behind her.

One of her ankle ribbons got caught in the door. Dandelion heard Olga shriek and fall. Olga opened the door again and yanked on the offending ribbon. Her face, beneath her feathers, had turned purplish-red, from embarrassment or anger, Dandelion didn't know which. Olga scrunched up her glowering face and spat.

She banged the door shut a second time, as loud as she could.

*Mocking somebird else's appearance is a surefire way
to make yourself feel beautiful.*
—FROM THE BOOK OF HERESY

5
PAIN IN PAINTING

In the darkness of a deeper night, Dandelion pressed her cool, smooth birthday candle against her face. But thoughts invaded her mind and wouldn't let her sleep.

She realized now, injured as she was, that she could not go home herself; yet why hadn't her mother and father come to her?

But of course, she thought. They couldn't. Mama and

Papa belonged far away in the valley, unable to come up to the mountain to rescue her, because a weaver and a hunter would not be allowed into the Castle of Sky. She would have to wait until her wings healed, and then she could go home to them.

In the nights, she dreamed of gliding down the mountain, and into a magical valley, and into the wings of her mother. She wept silent tears all night long in her sleep, but awoke convinced that it was dew.

Hours blurred into days, days into weeks, for Dandelion, trapped on her sickbed. Fleydur visited every day. But while he was not there, Olga, with narrowed eyes, set about making Dandelion as miserable as possible, determined to make Dandelion pay for her humiliation.

Olga dumped vinegar in Dandelion's soup and made loud, biting comments about her to nobird in particular. And then Fleydur, the only golden eagle who cared about her, stopped his visits. It was said that he was busy outside on the mountain, so Olga grew even bolder. She did not starve Dandelion, thinking it no fun, but meticulously prepared nasty surprises. Once she brought a piece of bricklike burned toast for Dandelion to eat, spread thick with rancid yellow soap. Seeing Dandelion choke and gag was not enough. She shoved the remains under Dandelion's bed when Dandelion was asleep, so when the housekeeper charged in a week later to investigate odd smells, Olga conveniently blamed it on Dandelion's "valley odor."

When will I be able to walk and go back home? Dandelion wondered each night.

One morning while Olga was away for her lessons, the physician marched into her room with a pair of steel scissors, snipped through Dandelion's bandages, and untied her splints. "Sit up! Then tell me if you feel strong enough to walk," he said cheerily, tossing off a piece of linen. Dandelion blinked and cautiously emerged from the bandages as if from a second eggshell. She scrambled up, and stood, swaying, on her feet. "Yes!" she cried. Her wings felt barely hinged—it was too soon for flying, but it was better than lying down waiting for Olga's tortures. She'd run and run—

Another eagle appeared in the doorway, blocking her way. "You are expected someplace. I am Uri, Prince Fleydur's valet. He has instructed me to take you to the tutor."

"Tutor?" Dandelion cried, horrified. The tutor taught Olga. She didn't want to see Olga. What would Olga say when she saw Dandelion in class with her? There were all these complications. Couldn't they understand? All a little eaglet wanted was to learn how to fly, and go home.

But perhaps . . . "Will I learn how to fly in class?" she asked.

Uri looked amused. "Not this class. Concerned with the higher functions of the mind, or so they say."

That Fleydur hadn't told her about this made her a little anxious. *But it's temporary,* she assured herself as the valet led her down a spiral staircase and along an empty corridor.

Uri stopped before a wooden door, rapped, and opened it. "Simplicio!" he called.

An absolutely ancient eagle teetered out of the room, shutting the door behind him. He wore a black courtier cap and a starchy robe, its severity only diminished by an eye-catching speck of dried spittle on the front.

"Fleydur has told you she will be in your class?" asked Uri.

"He has," Simplicio the tutor croaked. "The valley fledgling, my pupil?" He shook his head. "She hasn't enough knowledge, no skill. No qualifications at all. She is no duchess, no lady, no daughter of a noble! But she may *meet* the eaglets here, I suppose. Ought not to be too much of a bad influence. All right then. Come in. You have met Miss Olga already. One of my best students in etiquette, very polite and proper." Simplicio opened the door, pushing Dandelion inside.

All the heads whipped in unison over to look at her, their collective gaze like a stinging slap. Dandelion shut her beak tightly. The curtains of the tall windows in the classroom were drawn half closed, so she did not see much detail in their faces, only their brown mirrors of eyes, peering over a sea of rectangular easels. They perched on stools in fan-shaped rows. An empty stool had been placed in the center of the hard tiled floor, next to a lantern that cast a halo of glaring light.

"Today we are painting," the tutor explained. "Class, we have a new pupil." He nodded to the eaglets, who were still staring, transfixed.

"Who's she?" a short, pudgy male eaglet in the front row shouted, pointing at her with a dripping paintbrush.

"My name is Dandelion," she answered.

"I can't hear you, what title is that? Speak up!" the eaglet taunted her.

"Oh, don't be silly, Pudding." Olga spoke from the back row. "She has no title."

During the awkward silence, Simplicio shut his classroom door. "If you'd like to know, Master Pouldington, Dandelion is from the valley. She has just recovered from terrible injuries; that is why she is here at all. I hope you will treat her accordingly." Simplicio turned around. "Do you know how to paint, child? Laws of perspective, ratios, the balance of light and shadow?" Dandelion shook her head. "I thought not!" Simplicio clucked his tongue in satisfaction. "You will hardly be able to catch up."

Dandelion was rooted to the spot, not knowing what to do and feeling hopelessly awkward. She did not spy any empty seat in the rows of painting eaglets. There was no extra easel. Olga made a face at her and Pudding still stared at her.

"She can be the model!" Pudding called. Olga screeched in agreement. "We can paint her today, and she'll just sit there!" He pointed to the brightly lit, lonely stool in front of everybird.

"Excellent. That will do. Come, child." Simplicio clapped his wings, pushing Dandelion to the seat. "It's quite an honor for you. To my knowledge, most valley birds never get a portrait of themselves painted in their lifetimes." Tittering came from the class. Dandelion perched on the stool, the wood hard and cold in her talons. Simplicio fussed over the position of her wings, the tilt of her head, and then arranged the lantern till the light beamed to his satisfaction. For once, Dandelion yearned to have the bandages back to hide her body.

"Yes, class, this is a fine specimen of a valley bird. I expect your paintings will fully reflect the differences between the appearance of the golden eagles on the mountaintop and those in the valley. Pay attention to the darker coloring of her plumage. Anything else, do you see? Yes, Master Pouldington."

"They have a hulky, bulky body but a tiny head." Pudding said. Olga whooped out loud. Giggles came from other birds hiding their faces behind their easels. "They have squarish beaks and swollen feet." Pudding lifted a talon and wiggled his toes to demonstrate. Half the class again suppressed their laughter, while the other half waited for the tutor's reaction, though he rarely scolded the young noble, since Pudding's father, the treasurer, was the one who paid the tutor his wages.

Simplicio merely bleated, "Very observant, Master Pouldington. And Dandelion, please don't move."

Dandelion felt tears sting her eyes. "Why don't you look in a mirror!" she lashed back.

"Oh!" The breaths of the young nobility were one swift, hostile wind, flickering the lantern.

Simplicio stumbled toward her, a willow rod in his claws, his raspy voice rising in a screech like chalk on a blackboard. "I advise you, miss, to wash your beak of that mud of the uneducated. Speak properly to the son of the treasurer."

"But—"

"Enough!" Simplicio cried. "Life is not fair, and teachers are here to enforce that." The venerable tutor, so rickety in his movements, hit with startling deftness. *Whack! Whack! Whack!* Thrice, hard, across her talons. Her toes now really swelled.

She held back the burning tears. If they thought they could gloat over her tears, they would be disappointed. She sat painfully straight, faced off to one direction, the lantern illuminating her stiffness.

"If you stay, they're just going to make a fool of you. A valley fool." Olga's words rang in her ears. Olga, now, was smirking in amusement as she painted in the back row.

Tutor Simplicio weaved in and out of the rows of students, cackling, "Very good, very good!" like a gleeful merchant.

What in the mountain range makes them so terrible? And what is wrong with coming from the valley? Dandelion wondered. After all, it was the mountaintop that was uncomfortable—rocky, cold, barren, and ever so windy, while the valley bloomed and flowered, lush and green.

It is me, then? What's wrong with me?

Suddenly the quiet was broken by a small clatter, as if somebird had dropped a paintbrush. It came from the dark side of the room, but when she looked over in that direction, she just saw Pudding. The noise hadn't come from him. Pudding was busy adding rough, broad strokes to his artwork, a horrid look on his pudgy face. In the shadows next to him, somebird moved and straightened, looking directly at her with a familiar, friendly smile.

Her heart leaped, and for a moment she felt joyful. It was Cloud-wing! She hadn't noticed that he was in the class. Then a small doubt stirred in her—was he as nice as he had seemed to her before, or was he really just another spoiled young lord? Cloud-wing whispered some words to her, but she couldn't hear. Since she wasn't allowed to move, she blinked a few times.

"Mr. Simplicio?" Pudding spoke out again, loudly, holding his palette. "I have a question."

"Yes?" the tutor said.

"I painted next to her a scroll about the uses of manure in farming," Pudding announced. "But can valley eagles read?"

"No, of course not," said Simplicio crisply. "Get a scraper here, or some of this base paint, and cover it up!"

Cloud-wing frowned a little and watched carefully as Pudding squeezed himself out of his row. Cloud-wing hunched over and rapidly did something to Pudding's stool in the darkness.

The birds sitting behind Cloud-wing straightened, attentive, yet they kept curiously quiet. Dandelion was struck by a thought. Perhaps Cloud-wing was the son of a prestigious official as well, as high as Pudding's father, the treasurer, and lower-ranked court eaglets dared not offend them. Indeed, now that she was paying closer attention, she saw that Cloud-wing had four miniature gold acorns pinned around his collar, as did Pudding. Olga had only half an acorn pin.

So, the higher ranked the eaglets were, the more acorns pins they had *and* the closer they sat to the front, Dandelion decided. Olga, in the back, was not so important then, though she had put up such a grand facade. Then Dandelion noticed that there was a gap in the front row, where two or three stools might fit. *Places for the highest,* she thought. *Princes or princesses.* But neither Prince Fleydur nor Forlath had children. Dandelion looked back at Pudding's empty stool.

Oblivious, Pudding returned to his seat. Cloud-wing withdrew to his own painting. Pudding sat down, with a discernable *squish.* The birds nearby held their breaths.

Yet he showed no sign of noticing. The whole class was tense, as if on puppet strings.

When Simplicio hit the side of his desk with his cane, class was finally over. "Bring your canvases to me if you are finished," he called, drawing open the curtains of the room. The first to go up was Pudding. Everybird else stayed seated. Pudding held his painting aloft, immensely proud of himself as he ran up to display his work to the tutor.

"Oh!" Olga shrieked, bobbing her lace-capped head. "Look!"

Pudding's back was to the rest of the eaglets, and encrusted on the feathers of his behind was a huge circle of pink paint. The class erupted in laughter. "Look, a tutu!" And the son of the treasurer ran in circles, trying to see the pink paint, on his face a comical look of surprise.

Dandelion hopped off her stool and bolted outside. Cloud-wing brushed past her, smiling, and she tried to return his smile. He was clever and kind, trying to make her feel better, but it only made her suddenly realize how deeply wounded and confused and irritated she was. She left as quickly as she could and ran through the corridors, trying to hold back the emotions that now, when nobird was around, boiled over.

She sobbed with relief when she touched the crystal doorknob of her own door. Quickly she entered the room and shut the door behind her, leaning against the cool wood. *Nobird cares when somebird tramples upon dandelions. They're weeds, aren't they? And a tough dandelion doesn't cry.*

Nothing is something.
—FROM THE *BOOK OF HERESY*

6
BETWEEN MOTHER AND SON

O h, no. No, no, no," said a gruff female voice. "You'd think Fleydur would sit still, grateful that he's escaped death for returning. But it's been just a month, and he already itches to mold the mountain like clay." There was a sigh. "You know your father has never written a will and named his heir. When Fleydur was banished, you were the obvious choice for successor. But now Morgan confides in *him*, talking of reopening mines of generations ago, of allowing music, of other madness!"

Dandelion stumbled, alarmed. She had entered the wrong room. This was a small and dimly lit antechamber, and voices were coming from the crack of a door into an inner room. She must have gotten completely lost in the corridors and staircases. Dandelion was about to turn and leave but choked back a shout when the door she leaned on swept her into the wall.

Mashed in the tight space, she squirmed, her heart pounding. Whoever had entered remained standing in the entrance, his breathing audible.

"Message and delivery!" The voice boomed inches from her ear. "Here is a scroll from Fleydur to all of the court, outlining his desire to schedule a meeting with the Iron Nest."

"Thank you. I shall get it," said a familiar voice, Prince Forlath's. *Fleydur's brother!* Dandelion thought. *And the other eagle in the inner room, is she his mother, the queen? Where is Fleydur?* Forlath approached the messenger, but he continued his conversation with the queen. "Really, Mother, I feel that you're making a pebble into a mountain. It's no secret Fleydur wants to improve our kingdom. See, he is drafting a proposal."

As Forlath's clawsteps receded again, the queen

cleared her throat. "Oh, *is* that his intention? Is it really?"

As the messenger left, he jerked the door shut, exposing Dandelion.

She froze. The entrance to the inner chamber was wide open! Forlath's silhouette filled the doorway of the inner room. But his back was to her. "Fleydur's true intention? I do not know what you mean." Forlath's voice was slightly trembling.

"You know full well what I mean!" The gruff voice abruptly changed to a pleasant, ladylike tone. "Or do I have to put thoughts into your head as well as words, dear boy?"

"Mother, I do not—"

"Fleydur is here, trying to get at the throne!" The queen's voice was shrill.

"So what?" asked Forlath. "So what if Fleydur becomes king?"

Dandelion finally succeeded in prying the door open a crack. She slipped out of the room, running in the direction she had come from.

"What's that?" she heard Sigrid cry.

Did Forlath spin around and see her? Were claw-steps hurrying behind her? Dandelion didn't wait to find out. She tore into a side corridor, taking turns and twists whenever available, knowing that if they saw her, it would only take a few beats to overtake her on wing.

Oh, if I could fly now! she thought.

To her alarm, a bird ambled around the corner just ahead. She skidded to a halt, ready to spin around, but it was none other than the physician who had checked on her earlier in the morning.

"There you are, Dandelion," the physician said. "I could not find you in your room. I was beginning to wonder if the castle walls had swallowed you up."

"I got lost." She panted, keeping an attentive ear for any sound of clawsteps behind her. There seemed to be none.

"There, there," said the physician, patting her head. "This place does seem to spawn new corridors when your back is turned. But it's all right now." He gestured for her to turn around. "Come, quickly."

Dandelion sighed in relief. "Thank you, sir," she said. They walked in the direction she'd come from. She couldn't wait to be inside the safety of her room and figure out her next step—how to find Fleydur. "I didn't mean to be troublesome," she added.

The physician led her around a corner. "Not at all. I don't suppose you'd find the queen's chamber by yourself anyhow."

Dandelion stumbled to a stop. "What?" She must have heard wrong.

"We are going to Her Majesty Queen Sigrid's drawing room. Did I forget to tell you this morning?" he answered cheerfully, assuming Dandelion's wide eyes and open beak were signs of awe. "For some days now, she has been looking forward to conversing with you privately." He gestured to the door he'd stopped in front of. It was the door she'd fled through only minutes ago.

"Why?" Dandelion cried, edging backward. The door was shut tight, as if the queen's conversation with Forlath hadn't happened at all.

"The queen wants to get to know you, I believe."

"Can't I go back to my room right now, please, sir?"

"Oh, don't be shy. The queen is a sensitive and caring lady."

With that, the physician opened the door and shoved Dandelion in.

The door to the room beyond the antechamber was still open, and Dandelion could see inside. The windows were flung wide, the curtains open to let afternoon sunshine pour in. Forlath, it seemed, had left.

"Come in."

Sigrid's eyes were black, shot with flecks of gold. Her

feathers shimmered with yellow powder. She lifted a set of talons to motion to her hummingbird handmaid, and Dandelion noticed that Sigrid's toenails were filed to sharp points and painted bloodred.

The hummingbird brought a plate of cookies to Dandelion.

If the queen gives me a cookie, she can't have seen me, Dandelion thought, and picked a small one.

"Pour some tea for the child, too," Sigrid said to her handmaid as she got up and walked to her window. "Whoever do you think was listening at my door a moment ago? I feel it was Fleydur. Thinking he's so sly and clever. He can't even talk to me face-to-face!"

Dandelion nearly dropped her cookie.

"Or maybe it was his valet. It shows how uncouth Fleydur is. He puts up one face for the court, but inside, he's plotting something else altogether. I don't care how much he's overheard. I don't care what he would do about it—"

"He didn't!" Dandelion said.

Sigrid turned around, huge and frightening in her regalia. Ornate lace-edged sleeves only emphasized her bulk as she towered over Dandelion.

"Fleydur didn't listen," Dandelion whispered.

"Why do you vouch for him, sweetie?" said the queen.

Does she know? Does she know? Dandelion's mind was paralyzed by fear. Sigrid didn't wait for her answer.

"Does he treat you so well? Is that it?" Sigrid ventured. "I'm puzzled why he would. Come closer," she said. "My eyes are not as good as they once were. I cannot see you well."

Sigrid's strong clutch pulled Dandelion forward till they were nearly beak to beak.

"A true valley child," Sigrid said. "Your feathers, not golden, not caramel, not mahogany, not coffee, not chocolate—just about jet black. A whole bathtub of gold cosmetic powder wouldn't lighten that up." Sigrid cackled.

Dandelion tried to break away. "Fleydur is good to me because he is kind," she protested.

"Is he?" Sigrid took a sip of tea.

The calm before the storm, Dandelion thought.

"Do you know why Fleydur was exiled in the first place?" asked the queen. "A good, virtuous bird isn't threatened with the sentence of death if he returns, for nothing."

Dandelion shook her head.

"It was for his music and his attitude. In the beginning, Fleydur was restless and secretive, sometimes slipping into the treasury, other times disappearing from

Sword Mountain for hours at a time."

Sigrid banged her teacup on the table at the memory. "Who finally caught him fooling around with one of the kingdom's most important treasures? Me. Then Morgan suspected Fleydur of stealing funds for the enemy, but I knew Fleydur was dabbling in music. When the court investigated where Fleydur sneaked off to, who decided to follow him? Me, with my courtier Simplicio. For the greater good of the mountain, I hardened my heart and went to spy on the stepson I had raised. It was I who presented the indisputable evidence that earned him his exile!"

Dandelion saw a terrible mixture of pain and pride on Sigrid's face.

"We caught him squawking 'songs' with coarse beggars. It was shameful! Yet when I listened to the words, I knew that the ideas swarming in his mind were more dangerous than the tunes themselves." Sigrid pointed at Dandelion. "Now that you're healed, I can tell he's up to something again. That's why I summoned you here. I know what he's conspiring to do has to be bigger than getting the right to sing, but I cannot lay my talon on it."

"But I barely see him, Your Majesty," said Dandelion carefully.

"You silly child!" All vestiges of courtesy disappeared from Sigrid's face. "Still backing Fleydur, are you? He's sly enough to save you, so you are obliged to be grateful to him; he's even slyer to bring you here, where every-bird else loathes you, so you'll stay loyal to him. Do you think he cares for you? He cut himself off from family values, long ago. But I," she said, "I am a mother." She set down her teacup with finality. "Let me know then if Fleydur acts strangely. Come to me, and for every report of Fleydur you give me, I will give you flight lessons."

At that moment Dandelion remembered a nugget of truth about Fleydur's thoughtfulness that made her doubt the queen. "Fleydur wished me happy birthday. He sang me 'Happy Birthday.'"

Sigrid recoiled.

"He lies," she whispered. "Ask him about when you'll see your parents again. Watch him stall. Watch him lie."

The hummingbird opened the door for Dandelion.

Dandelion discovered the physician several corridors away, chatting with a guard. "Wonderful day for you, isn't it, Dandelion? Going to school and meeting the queen?" he said. "And the housekeeper brought new dresses for you, too, courtesy of the Castle of Sky; now won't you like that?" He led her back toward her room.

Dandelion said her thanks and followed. Deep in her

thoughts, she didn't notice when the physician left and she entered her sickroom.

"Dandelion? What's wrong? How did your classes go?" Dandelion jumped as she saw that Fleydur himself was sitting in the room in the noon warmth, waiting. It was his first visit in several weeks now. A smile graced his face.

"I don't want to return to the tutor's class," said Dandelion. "I want to see my parents. I want to go home."

"I will personally bring you to your family's cave someday. But now we need to take care of you, too," he said. "Why don't you want to go to class with Simplicio?"

"I'm a valley weed," she said, and shut her beak and inspected her feet.

Fleydur paused at this, frowning. "You don't need to go to Simplicio's class, then," he said gently. "Dandelion. Look at me. You are fine the way you are, understand?" His words were quiet and deliberately restrained, but Dandelion could see his feathers quivering. *He cares,* she thought. Anxious that she sounded like a childish tattler, she tried to say something else. Stirring up trouble or making the prince do anything more for her was the last thing she wanted to do.

She thought of the queen. "Fleydur, I have something

important to tell you." Fleydur looked concerned. "When I got out of class, I got lost in the hallways and went into the wrong place. I thought it was here, the doors were so alike." She swallowed. "I went into a room and heard the voice of the queen. She sounded angry about you. Then later she actually talked to me and . . . I'm sorry, I'm so sorry, but Fleydur, you should be careful!"

To her horror, Fleydur relaxed, and he even gave a light laugh. "I was worried my mother had turned too sour for eaglets' company. She's got room in her heart for youngsters after all."

He shook his head merrily. "And nobird is going to say anything about you just because you accidentally went into the wrong room, Dandelion. And Sigrid, though hot-tempered and stubborn sometimes, gets along fine with me."

"But—"

"It doesn't matter." Fleydur shook his head again, as if trying to get Dandelion to understand something. "My own mother died of an illness when I was quite young," he said gently. "It was Sigrid who raised me all those seasons and preened my feathers when I had a fever. Her love for me and her love for the mountain show in different ways."

Dandelion closed her beak. He made her sound

unreasonable, suspecting one's own mother, and for a moment she felt absurd. *Could the queen be right?* Dandelion contemplated the thought. Fleydur had been kind to her, but could he have had some ulterior motive, as Sigrid had claimed? Did Dandelion truly know what the prince was like? *He was young once,* she thought. *He had a tutor. He was a prince who sat in those empty places in the front row of the class.* Was Fleydur a Cloud-wing or a Pouldington?

Fleydur looked sad. "If you were wondering, I think I know why my mother would be so agitated about me."

"Does it have something to do with why you've been away so much?"

"Yes. I plan to create a special school on Sword Mountain. I've submitted the proposal, and I will hear from the court tomorrow. They call themselves the Iron Nest, guarding the egg of the mountain's future . . . iron mind-sets, more like, I fear. We need a special place, a refuge from the likes of Simplicio, where birds like you can be happy."

Dandelion realized that Fleydur was almost an outsider with his views, well meaning but misunderstood. He was a Dandelion.

"Oh, prince," she said in a small voice. "But you—"

"Don't worry about me, Dandelion," Fleydur said.

We flock together when we share the inner plumage of the soul.
—FROM THE *OLD SCRIPTURE*

7
BIRDS OF A FEATHER

F leydur was walking down the staircase from the king's tower when a whisper flew at him from the evening darkness.

"Fleydur!"

"It is you, Forlath?" he said, straining his eyes.

"Yes." His brother glided up from a lower landing.

"Why are you about at this hour?" asked Fleydur.

"Looking for you," said Forlath. "Why are you?"

"Father called me in," he said simply.

A glumness, like a dew-weighted spiderweb, hung in the dark gap between the two brothers. Fleydur listened to Forlath's breathing: in and out, in and out. . . .

"How is Father? He hasn't talked to me the past few days," said Forlath.

"He's better," said Fleydur.

"Good," said Forlath. But Fleydur knew he had something more in his heart. Somehow it seemed that Forlath was afraid to say what had prompted him to come searching for Fleydur in the first place.

Fleydur decided to ease the awkwardness. "I haven't seen you much either. Haven't been at the castle," he said.

"You haven't been," agreed Forlath. "Mother was thinking over it." And Fleydur sensed a tenseness that he had never associated with his younger brother before.

"I see," said Fleydur. "Want to go up to the base of Sword Cliff? Just like the old days, nobird but us two."

Sword Cliff, that pillar pointing to the sky, seemed to be waiting for the two brothers to come to its base. From afar it looked a needle in the night, sewing stars into the sky. Once below it, however, its size and magnificence brought to mind a sacred staircase bridging the world above to the mortal world below.

At first Fleydur and Forlath spoke no word but simply gazed at the cosmos, feeling the wind ruffle their feathers.

"Tell me, Fleydur. What have you been doing?" asked Forlath at last.

"I'm going to . . . build a conservatory, a music school, on Sword Mountain," said Fleydur.

"A *music* school?" Forlath's voice shook as if discussing contraband. "What do you mean for it to do?"

"Change things," said Fleydur. "I will go where no eagle has ever dared to go before: anybird of any species, of any tribe, can attend if they love music, for free! It's a school where a valley eaglet won't feel bad. And once there are birds here who know how to sing, they will be able to use the Leasorn gem to summon Swordbird, the hero who helps others in need. I've already located building materials, found a good place midslope, and I've sneaked a load of music instruments into my room. I've submitted the paperwork. I just need official approval."

But Forlath wasn't listening. "Anybird can attend?" he repeated. He squinted in the dark at Fleydur's face, to see if he was serious. "You know what that implies? Great Spirit, Fleydur."

"Father allows music, didn't he say so?"

"A song or two, yes. Not a whole school. You can't. The court, the Iron Nest, will raise havoc! And my mother will be furious, aghast."

"I've traveled enough to know that this is what Sword Mountain sorely needs."

"But your plan would defy nearly a chapter in the *Handbook of the Feathered Aristocrat.*"

"What, you too, Forlath? The dotards who print that book spend their days cultivating a protruding stomach rather than a logical mind!" Fleydur threw open his wings. "Tell me, what wrong have I done? You tried to stop me from saving Dandelion, and now—"

"No," said Forlath, pained. "We're just . . . we aren't ready for radical changes like this, Fleydur. Not yet."

Fleydur stepped away, his sides heaving in the darkness.

Forlath followed. "Fleydur, listen to me. I am your brother, not your enemy. I've been at home ruling on Father's behalf all these years you were away, and I understand the court better than you do," he whispered. "Your dreams, they're too idealistic for our kingdom. You can't tackle all the injustices of the world."

Forlath squatted besides Fleydur. "I think your vision of a music school—well, it's like flying, Fleydur. We need to test the air and trust it before we dare to soar. Think of something smaller, Fleydur. Something to convince the court that your dreams are valid, so they can dare to let go and take the plunge."

Early next morning, Dandelion, holding her candle, peeked through the curtains at the swirling clouds below her window. She'd waited long enough. Her bandages were gone, and her wings, though scarred, were healed. It was time to teach herself to fly.

She tucked her candle into her pocket and beat her wings as hard as she could. The second her talons rose from the carpet, though, her heart hammered, out of rhythm. A chain of images started in her mind, and once again, the archaeopteryx slashed. . . . Her mother, screaming in outrage, struck back, and the two, locked together, fell in an arc and the archaeopteryx suddenly turned to . . .

The strange, inhibiting fear yanked Dandelion down again; for a moment she could not breathe and could not see. As she picked herself up from the ground where she had fallen, she sickened to think she was rebelling against herself. She'd outwit her fears. Now.

Dandelion left her room and walked along the corridor till she arrived at a staircase. Twenty steps led to the landing below. She took a step back, and then dived.

For a split second, Dandelion was flying—

"What are you doing!" screeched Olga as they collided. The teacup she was holding flew high in the air; an arc of amber tea cascaded down to douse them both. Dandelion crashed onto the banister and slid down another flight of stairs before she could stop herself.

"Ooh, you! Come back here, you!" Olga was leaning over the railing, tea dripping from between her narrowed eyes.

Dandelion stumbled up the stairs, dismayed. "I'm so sorry, Olga," she said. "I was trying to fly. I didn't see you coming up around the landing."

"You never do anything but cause trouble," said Olga.

"Me?" said Dandelion, aghast. "Olga! I didn't mean to collide with you. I'll go get the physician if you need him. I'll get you some more tea. Really, I'll make up for it. What can I do for you?"

Olga closed her beak. And blinked. "Anything?" she said.

"Anything," Dandelion agreed.

Olga's smile turned into an ugly smirk. "Good."

She dragged Dandelion up the stairs and down a corridor. She went into a room and reappeared with a rose-scented envelope under one wing. "You'll deliver a letter for me to Master Golden, the general's son," she instructed. "Say to him, 'My lady, Miss Olga, sincerely wishes Master Golden the best of luck in his examinations!' Okay?"

"Sure," said Dandelion slowly.

"And it'll be perfect. He'll be charmed by my letter, and he'll see that you're really fit to be nothing but a servant," Olga said.

Dandelion was not sure who Olga was talking about. But she'd made her promise, and it was best to carry out the task in good will.

"Well, don't loiter. Hurry, before the examinations start!"

"What examinations?" Dandelion asked.

"The entrance examinations for the Rockbottom Academy. You know, the martial arts school way over on Double Pain Peak. They're this afternoon."

"But wait, Olga," Dandelion said. "I hardly know where to look for this eagle! I can't find my way around in the castle at all."

"Everybird knows who Golden is and where he goes," said Olga, shrugging. "Just ask whoever you see."

Olga was not wrong. Golden was a magical word that animated old and young alike. To her alarm, every young female eaglet Dandelion came across giggled incessantly at the mention of his name. Older matrons sighed as if contemplating an ideal son. The castle staff and the guards nodded in admiring approval; one emotional bird even raised a cup of wine on the spot and toasted Golden. *How miraculous,* Dandelion marveled. *A bird loved by everybird!*

What was more, everybird seemed eager to mention something about him, unprompted.

"He is going to finish first in the exams," one said. "The pride of Sword Mountain, he is!"

"Had he been the son of one of the princes, he would be a marvelous ruler someday," cried another.

"He's *so* charming!" cooed a third.

Is he perfect? thought Dandelion. *I hope he isn't proud or haughty.* She was directed to the walled courtyard at the back of the castle. Some boys were there, practicing martial arts to prepare for tryouts later in the afternoon. Dandelion watched and waited, apprehensive.

Many of the eaglets wore leather armor; some had helmets with flaps that hid their faces. The sunlight flashing from their swords dazzled her, at first reminding her of the attacking archaeopteryx. But these eaglets' movements weren't crude or threatening; they were strong, synchronized, sweeping, like a dance.

She was fascinated by how secure the eaglets looked, for they knew how to defend themselves and their family against any armed foe. They needn't hide or flee, scream or be helpless. They could rise up and meet an attacker readily. If only that was something she could do! She'd have to fly, too, of course, but if she could only fly *and* wield a sword like that.

When practice was over, Dandelion walked to the nearest eaglet and told him of her search, and he called over one of the birds who was fully armored.

"Somebird asking for me?" said Golden, taking off his helmet.

Dandelion looked up and was astounded.

"What?" she gasped. "Golden? Cloud-wing? You're Golden?"

Tawny-feathered Cloud-wing looked embarrassed. "That's what they all call me. But I'd rather you call me Cloud-wing. It's my real name, after all."

"But why don't the others call you Cloud-wing?" asked Dandelion, curious.

"Don't know," mumbled Cloud-wing. Even his embarrassed grimace was a perfectly likable grimace. "Guess they can't see past my feathers," he added.

Dandelion understood. In reality, golden eagles weren't golden but came in a palette of browns. Some even had plumage that was as dark as valley earth, like Dandelion herself.

Although all had at least a patch of tawny feathers on the back of their necks that justified the name, it was the goal of fashionable golden eagles to appear as "gold" as possible. Some wore dark blue scarves to bring out a yellower hue. Those who could afford it sported plenty of gold jewelry and cufflinks. The immensely wealthy, like the queen, sprinkled a metallic powder on their wings and faces.

But among the nobility, there were lucky families of birds whose feathers had just the "right" color. Cloud-wing came from such a family. He fairly glowed.

"What's wrong with Golden, though?" asked Dandelion.

"How'd you feel if you were called perfect and golden all the time?" Cloud-wing said.

"I don't know," said Dandelion. "I'd be very glad at first, I guess."

Cloud-wing nodded.

"But it's pretty tough keeping up with perfect," Dandelion went on after a pause. "I guess you lose yourself."

"See? That's what I mean. You understand." He waved a wing impulsively. "Isn't it funny, I could send others reeling if I told them I planned to dye my feathers dark. You're the only one I bet who won't."

"I won't. But," she said, thinking further, "you don't believe that my feather color is what makes me think one way or another, do you?"

"No! Great Spirit, what a stupid thing I said. I was trying to say you understand me because you're like me," said Cloud-wing. A look of relief flooded his face.

"Like you?" Dandelion was shocked. He nodded. "I'm miles away from even being acceptable here!"

"No, don't you see, Dandelion?" said Cloud-wing. "Others call you a valley bird and take for granted you're slow-witted and clumsy, when you obviously aren't. They don't see who you really are. They see a country bumpkin. As for me—they think I'm perfect, and I tell them I'm not. But they don't believe me, and cry that I am wonderfully modest. All they see is Golden—an ideal eaglet of their dreams. They don't see *me*. Cloud-wing doesn't exist."

"Rubbish. That was definitely Cloud-wing, not Golden, making that speech," said Dandelion.

Cloud-wing smiled faintly.

"Still," Dandelion added, "I think being thought of as perfect is a little more endurable than being thought of as a peasant."

"Is it?" he whispered.

The two eaglets looked into each other's face. Each wondered, for a split second, whether the other was a mirror image, even though the two looked nothing alike.

"Although others make assumptions about your so-called perfection, they still support you," said Dandelion. "They give you confidence, so you can take on tough tasks, like learning to fly, and—"

"Wait," said Cloud-wing. "Can't you fly?"

Dandelion shook her head.

"Then I'll support you," Cloud-wing said. "I'll teach you how. There's enough time yet before my examinations. I'm going to get something you'll need to fly. Meet me at the boulders outside the castle."

"Why?"

"Why not? It'll be an adventure of sorts."

Dandelion thanked him and was about to turn when he called to her.

"Dandelion? I'm sorry about the way Pudding and the others acted. They . . . they don't know any better," Cloud-wing said. "But I hope you will stay awhile on the summit."

She couldn't believe her ears. Though touched, Dandelion knew she needed to return home as soon as she could. She remembered Olga's rose-scented envelope and presented it to him. His eyes widened.

"Olga," said Dandelion hastily. "Er . . . My lady, Miss Olga, sincerely wishes Master Golden the best of luck in the examinations!"

"Thanks . . . tell her thanks," Cloud-wing said politely, but added, "Why are you running her errands? She's your companion, she's supposed to make sure you're okay."

Dandelion took a deep breath and walked down a corridor. She supposed she'd better tell Olga that her note had been delivered before going outside for her flight lesson. The corridor wound into the interior of the castle. Instead of windows, there were rows of mirrors on the walls, hung between torches.

All sorts of mirrors were there: round, square, silver, copper, most of them framed by painted wood, some with a rosy or blue tint, others uneven so that they would distort the viewer's image.

She stopped in front of one that had a metal plate over it: FLIGHT MIRROR. It was so wide it allowed birds to see every feather of their wingspan. *What will flight look like for me?* Curious, Dandelion unfurled her wings before it. Her wings filled up the frame, grand in their symmetry, so that she seemed five times bigger. The feathers that had frayed from her fall gave her the air of a flight veteran already. Dandelion lifted her wings up and down, angling them as if in a dive, imagining herself listening to every wind's whisper, as the sky's confidante.

Dandelion was not the only one to be fascinated. As she continued on the corridor, she found Olga slouching dreamily in front of a sheet of glass labeled BEAUTY MIRROR.

The mirror had a floral-design frame and was tinted gold. As Olga gazed into her lighter, yellower reflection, she breathed toward the glass, and on the fogged surface, she rubbed the shape of a heart. With every inhale, the heart faded away, and with every exhale, Olga redrew the heart.

Perhaps it would be best, Dandelion thought, not to tell Olga about her letter after all.

Olga didn't notice Dandelion as she slipped quietly past. Dandelion glanced back once and saw, alone in that shining section of the corridor, Olga continuing her endless drawings of hearts.

Flight: It is your escape, yet it is your destiny.
—FROM THE OLD SCRIPTURE

8
ALOFT

With a foot suspended over the edge of the
cliff, Dandelion asked, "So I won't fall?"

Cloud-wing adjusted the compli-
cated straps that looped around her wings and over her
back, opened her bulky new backpack, and pulled out
white folds.

"You'll never even notice," he said. "The parachute
will buoy you up!"

"All right. One . . . two . . . three . . . !" Dandelion sprang from the edge as Cloud-wing flung the backpack behind her. She spread her wings wide, and with a *poof*, a great white parachute billowed above her, her very own cloud. She imaged herself a dandelion seed, out in the crisp mountain air.

Oh, my! Dandelion thought. And she had shaken her head in disbelief when Cloud-wing first thrust the pack at her. "It's an army parachute; my father let me borrow it so long as I don't tear it," he had said. "In battles the wounded use them, to help them stay aloft as they steer themselves to a healer's station."

"Move your wings to go left or right!" Cloud-wing now called, launching himself in the air to follow Dandelion.

Encouraged, Dandelion focused on flapping her wings, but the parachute that had supported her now resisted her efforts to move forward. At the mercy of the wind, she floated farther away, where she was swiftly caught in a gust that had funneled through narrow mountain passes.

"Cloud-wing!" she shouted as the wind hurled her backward, faster and faster, lower down the mountain. Dandelion glanced behind her to see a line of trees.

Crack! The parachute caught in the branches of a pine

tree. Dandelion flapped her wings as hard as she could to free herself, but the harnesses tangled even more and she heard a loud rip. And so she hung there, miserably, swinging back and forth, covered with pine needles.

"Where are you, Dandelion?"

"Here!" she said. "Please, help me. I'm in the tree!"

When Cloud-wing had loosened her harness and gotten her down, they both gazed up at the ruined parachute, limp above their heads. Though she could not really fly in the contraption, Dandelion felt tears in her eyes to see it ruined.

"But that was worth it," Cloud-wing was saying. "What a sight. And what fun!"

"You'll get in trouble." Dandelion was worried, but Cloud-wing merely said, "I'll take whatever punishment comes." He retrieved the remnants of the parachute.

In the distance, a drumroll sounded.

"That's the call for tryouts!" Cloud-wing jumped with a start. "I have to go to Rockbottom—".

"Then give the parachute to me, Cloud-wing," Dandelion said. "Let me try to fix it, and you can get it after your exams."

Back in her room, the huge white cloth spread over her bed, Dandelion studied the parachute. In the backpack of the harness, she had found white thread and a large needle.

She hadn't flown this evening, but she had jumped with a parachute filled with hope. And she had found a friend. The thought made her smile. Dandelion bent, crawling from one edge of the parachute to the other, the large needle flashing like a miniature sword in her claws as she pulled and mended. Sewing together her parachute. Sewing together her dreams.

When the sun glowed red and warm among the western peaks, Cloud-wing fluttered outside her window, tapping on the glass.

"Dandelion!"

Dandelion opened the window. He landed on the sill. "How did your entrance exams go?" she asked.

Cloud-wing winced. "Great, except I'm sure I failed. I had to do a triple back flip and I barely managed."

"Meaning you got in." Dandelion laughed.

"I don't know for sure," said Cloud-wing. "The results won't be announced till two weeks later. But I think everybird did all right, except Pudding. He doesn't try; he doesn't really want to be a warrior, anyway." Cloud-wing shrugged.

Dandelion remembered the pudgy bully. "But what

will his father think if he failed?"

"It doesn't matter to Mr. Pouldington Senior," said Cloud-wing. "And Pudding's older brother is one of the best at Rockbottom, anyway. It's an honor for even one of the family to get in—anybird in the Skythunder mountain range can apply to it, so there's fierce competition."

"Anybird?" asked Dandelion. "Even those from the valleys?"

"Y-yes." Cloud-wing looked stricken. "I mean, any young male bird of prey who is fairly able-bodied," he mumbled, embarrassed by his mistake.

Not girls, Dandelion realized. Rockbottom would take a valley boy—but not a valley girl.

"It's a military school, after all," Cloud-wing added lamely. He wanted to move away from the topic as quickly as possible, Dandelion could tell. "Anyway . . . flight," he said.

At this, Dandelion grabbed the backpack and harness and handed it over, showing Cloud-wing how the parachute, neatly folded within, had been put back together airtight.

"Oh, Dandelion, I thought of something—simpler. It might work better than the parachute. You could really fly today."

He pulled out a length of rope.

"What am I supposed to do?" Dandelion just stood dumbfounded as Cloud-wing offered her one end of the rope. How could an ordinary rope be a match for the pull of gravity?

Cloud-wing did not appear worried. "Hold on to this and don't let go. I'm at the other end. And we'll jump together, and we'll fly!"

Dandelion gripped the end, shaking her head. "But . . . but I'll just plummet like a ripe old apple off the branch! And you'll be dragged—"

"No, I'll be here, at the other end of the rope, and I'll hold you up," said Cloud-wing. "What have you got to fear?"

Dandelion squeezed the rope. "Then let's go," she said.

She climbed on the windowsill, and for a moment the two eaglets teetered at the edge. Dandelion stared at the clouds below her, crawling on the invisible surface of the atmosphere; the rays of the setting sun at that moment slanted, and all the windows of the castle were ablaze. The wind touched her talons, whispering for them to uncurl; buffeted her feathers, her wings; and she felt suddenly alive, alive for flight!

"You'll walk on the clouds!" Cloud-wing shouted.

A single breeze blew toward her, and she walked

forward into open air, wings raised high as if to embrace the whole world below. Cloud-wing was right beside her. For one chilling second she realized she was spinning down, and the rope went taut in her grasp. A rock formed in the pit of her stomach. She felt much more exposed than she had in the parachute, much more breakable.

"Relax! Close your eyes, ride the wind, don't grasp at it," Cloud-wing cried from above, fanning his wings as Dandelion dangled from the other end of the rope. "I'm here."

Dandelion forced herself to close her eyes.

She adjusted her wings to suit the wind, becoming a buoy in the ocean. She had it! For a second, she had it. She rose back up in the air, the rope fell slack, and she looked up at the grinning face of Cloud-wing.

Being airborne felt so fragile. If Dandelion were to let go of her breath, she felt that whatever it was that held her in the air would disappear. Hadn't her mother told her that she needed a special force to defy gravity and soar? Dandelion knew she herself had none of the power. It came from Cloud-wing—his compassion, confidence, and courage coursing through the rope and lending a moment of magic to her wings. She knew she would never fall with Cloud-wing holding on.

"See?" Cloud-wing said. His eyes sparkled. "How does it feel to fly?"

Dandelion didn't have to answer. There was a candle glow in her heart.

Cloud-wing beamed. "We're just hovering now. There's lots more to see!"

Dandelion was amazed. "Go farther out? I'm not sure if I can stay aloft that long." The archaeopteryx scars on her shoulders began to ache.

"Just a little more," he assured her. "We can have more lessons, but you've been here for weeks, and you haven't had a proper tour of the Castle of Sky."

He pointed to each of the four towers crowning the castle. "The north one, facing the wind, is the king and queen's. Their chamber and his workroom are there. The south tower is Prince Fleydur's study. The eastern tower is Forlath's. The western tower is the watchtower, where the soldiers go, to look out from the heart of the mountain range."

Only the watchtower was lit. *Where has the royal family all gone?* thought Dandelion.

Cloud-wing pointed out the banquet halls, libraries, offices, the wing for guests, and the wing for the castle staff. Then, lowering his voice, he gestured at the foundations of the castle and told her of the dungeon.

"It just runs around the perimeter of the foundations, because kings past wanted the throne room in the center to sit upon stone and earth, not above criminals," he explained. "The dungeon walls are twice as thick as the rest of the castle, and damp with slime. There is not a single window."

"Is anybird shut in it now?" Dandelion asked.

"None, at least nobird we remember," he said. "It'd be awfully lonely, and a bird could be easily forgotten in that dark."

Dandelion shivered. She observed the castle again. Lights shone from many of the windows now. Dandelion noticed that Cloud-wing had overlooked one of the brightest. "And that?" she whispered.

"The windows of the audience chamber," Cloud-wing said. "The brightest room of all. It's where the Iron Nest holds its assembly."

It all clicked in Dandelion's mind.

Fleydur will ask the court to pass his proposal! she remembered. "Tonight Fleydur will be there," she said.

Music and poetry can't be repressed;
They're needed for birds to be whole.
Poetry's always the speech of the heart,
Music, the tongue of the soul.
—FROM A SONG IN THE OLD SCRIPTURE

9
CLASH OF WORDS

ssembly! Assembly!" called the herald into the antechamber. "Prince Fleydur is here to present his proposal."

Bang! Bang! Bang!

Some of the ancient advisers of Morgan resented Fleydur, similar to the way Olga resented Dandelion. But instead of banging doors, they banged books. Slamming down the heavy volumes some of them were pretending to read, the sixteen advisers tottered toward their usual places—readily seen because of a shiny hollow in the floorboards each had worn from standing in the same place year after year. To them, any change was like a burp, best surpressed as a matter of good taste. They glared at Fleydur, who stood alert in the center.

"Did you read the details about the music school he wants to build?" one whispered. "For the life of me, I cannot imagine how I am to suffer through all his unrealistic, nonsensical—"

"Hush—here's the king!"

The advisers straightened, standing in two rows like chess pieces upon the black-and-white floor.

"Good evening to all assembled," Morgan called to them, flying to perch on his metal throne. He was much recovered now, his once-frail body filled with new vigor. "We've reviewed your proposal, Fleydur. The Iron Nest has informed me, though, that they must question you."

The king had barely finished speaking when old wheezy Simplicio, the tutor, lumbered forward onto a new square, his feathers puffed. "Prince, your proposal is very . . . thought-provoking. No, just plain provoking!" the tutor declared. "You wrote that this music school will be a place where that valley child will be treated well.

Treated well? Do you mean that in my classroom I treat her poorly?"

Murmurings erupted among the advisers. The queen's eyes were fixed upon Fleydur's face.

Simplicio continued, "In my classroom, the purpose of education is to ensure that birds act according to their places! She is a valley child and should be treated like one. It has been so and will always be. It is tradition."

The members of the Iron Nest muttered loudly among themselves once more.

Morgan waved his scepter for silence. "Other questions, on other aspects of Fleydur's proposal?"

Simplicio panted for breath but was intent on continuing to be the spokesbird of the Iron Nest. "Yes, Your Majesty, I do have another point. No respectable, traditional eagles of the mountaintop will let their children enroll in a music school and forego a proper education under me."

Simplicio turned to Fleydur, waving a copy of his proposal. "'Birds from other places, of other species may enroll,' you also wrote. But strangers are not allowed on the mountaintop! Are you trying to bend another tradition?" Simplicio's spittle flew sideways.

"Indeed!" cried Sigrid.

By now, Simplicio had advanced another square,

almost face-to-face with Fleydur. Other advisers hunched nearby. The air grew warm and stifling from their collective breath.

"Sirs." Fleydur cleared his throat. "I understand your concerns. I come with changes to my proposals."

The members of the Iron Nest were frozen midfrown.

"We'll begin small." Fleydur looked at Forlath. "Instead of a whole school, I propose to have a small class, an experimental class. And it shall be for just the birds of the Skythunder mountain range."

All the scholars grimaced.

"For just birds of Sword Mountain."

Still grimaces.

"For just eagles of Sword Mountain." Grimaces and fainter frowns were half and half.

"For . . . mostly the eagles of the summit of Sword Mountain. That is, I hope to hold music lessons for the children of the court. Outside of the castle. Apart from their studying hours. Totally voluntary," said Fleydur.

"The duration?" thundered Simplicio.

"The class will not last the whole year. Not even a semester," said Fleydur. "It'll begin in fall, and end in winter." Fleydur took a deep breath. "The last lesson will be on the king's birthday. Students will put on a concert that evening during the traditional gala dinner, for the enjoyment of His Majesty and his guests. The day afterward, the court will immediately gather for a final decision on whether to allow a permanent music school."

The eagles of the court eyed him as if he had blurted something obscene.

After a moment of shock, Simplicio bellowed anew. "To let such foulness taint the sacred birthday of His Majesty!"

Morgan raised a wing. "I think we have knowledge enough of this new plan. Fleydur has made his proposal; let the Iron Nest decide." Morgan turned his face toward a great bronze balance in the middle of the court. It was shaped like an eagle in flight; from its open wings hung the scales, now empty. "Cast your votes, members of the Iron Nest."

This vote will show if I have been truly accepted back into Sword Mountain, thought Fleydur, watching the advisers walk over to the secretary, Amicus. Each dropped from within his sleeve a large cube of polished black stone. Fleydur knew that each adviser had a set of two such stones, which they retrieved after each voting session. One had YEA etched onto one side; the other had NAY. Now no words could be seen, as all advisers put their stones facedown. Those stones were old, very old. Though the king had the right to issue new voting stones, it was rare for new birds to be admitted to the Iron Nest; more often than not, the stones were the jealously guarded property of a few elite families, handed down from father to son.

Fleydur averted his eyes and hoped for the best. *Would eagles be willing to venture anew?* he thought. *Or is Sword Mountain still unchangeable?*

"And Your Majesty?" Amicus collected the stone from the last adviser and looked toward the king.

Morgan selected one of his purple stones, the king's voting stones, and passed it to the secretary. It was bigger than any of the sixteen advisers', for the king's vote was worth three.

"Your Majesty, members of the Iron Nest," murmured Amicus. He stepped to face the life-size figure of the copper eagle on the balance scale and began with the traditional words: "O founder eagle of our mountain, who sees truth and falsehood alike, show us which direction now the Skythunder tribe is to fly!"

So the weighing of the votes began.

For each vote, Amicus flipped the stone over for all to see, reading the inscription and placing it on the scales.

Fleydur couldn't help but gaze into the eyes of the bronze eagle—those fixed metal eyes that were blind and yet seemed to see—as the voice of the secretary droned:

"Nay . . . nay . . . nay . . ."

The scale on the left wing was for the yea stones, the one on the right for nay. And every time a voting stone was dropped, the flying bronze eagle tipped farther to the right.

Glancing out of the corner of his eye, Fleydur saw that Simplicio's eyes were scrunched shut in malicious delight. Beyond, Sigrid squinted intently.

A flicker lit the queen's eyes as Amicus paused and then uttered, "Yea." Fleydur looked around. Somebird in the Iron Nest had supported him! And not just one, either, it seemed. The votes became a string of mixed yeas and nays.

Fleydur stood mesmerized, watching the bronze eagle. The weight of the voting stones on each wing made the eagle tip drunkenly from side to side as if caught in a rough wind.

Then, quite suddenly, it was over. The court watched as the balance scale steadied itself.

For a moment, Fleydur thought that the line of the wings was parallel to the floor. But it was only a trick of the light—one wing tip sagged lower.

*Certain elderly conservative officials are like
hard cheese: As they age, some enjoy them more,
but others complain more of a stink.*
—FROM THE *BOOK OF HERESY*

10
A Gap in the Iron Nest

S even yeas, nine nays," boomed Amicus. He
turned and nodded gravely to all who were
present. Fleydur's heart collapsed.

But then the secretary spoke again. "The king's vote."
He picked up the purple stone in his talons and placed it
gently upon the left scale. The bronze eagle made a last
swerve.

Nobird swore or cried out. Nobird cheered.

Amicus cleared his throat uncomfortably. "So we have spoken. So the founder eagle has shown the path for flight. Your Majesty, members of the Iron Nest—Prince Fleydur's new proposal has passed."

Thank you, thought Fleydur to the anonymous supporters within the Iron Nest. *Thank you, Father.* He looked at the intrepid bronze eagle of the balance scale, those fierce, kindly eyes, the wide wings, and thought, *Thank you for watching over me.*

He scanned the birds around him. Forlath's and Morgan's heads were held high as they nodded and beamed; Sigrid's head was lowered as she studied her painted nails. Much more distraught were the advisers, who had broken from their formation and instead stood scattered across the black-and-white floor.

Simplicio's gaze burned as he met Fleydur's eyes. He charged out of the group, and Fleydur thought for a moment that the tutor was about to throw himself at him.

At the last moment, Simplicio veered toward Morgan. Like dropping a rotten piece of herring left in the sun, Simplicio whipped off his black courtier cap and dumped it at the feet of the king.

"What is this, Simplicio?" Morgan said sternly.

"I do not wish to hold my office as tutor any longer,

as it seems I am no longer capable of coping with these rather *startling* changes," Simplicio said, averting his face so that the king could not see his expression. His strained, trembling voice betrayed him nonetheless. "As a thoughtful tutor, passionate about my work, I have high fears that music shall drug the minds of our children." Simplicio punctuated his remark by hurling his voting stone beside his cap. "Eagles have always been sages and warriors, not *entertainers*. I refuse to stand by and witness the loss of our dignity. I resign."

"Those are your final words on this subject?" Morgan said.

"No! I mean to say . . . if Your Highness would allow me a few more, from my sincere heart?" Simplicio's head lifted. He had even managed to put on a neutral face.

"Speak what you like. Speak, and you are dismissed."

The feathers on Simplicio's agitated face rose. He spun toward Fleydur. "You befoul, begrime, besmear, bedaub, besmirch, *bespatter* the honor of eagles!" His voice rose to its chalkboard screech as he pointed a shriveled talon.

"Be quiet and begone!" bellowed Forlath.

Simplicio's face tightened, his beetle eyes blinking furiously. With a sweep of his robe, he gathered his dignity and waddled out of the court.

"Well, that was very rash," Queen Sigrid said with annoyance.

Simplicio left much more than a gap in the Iron Nest. Who would tutor the court children? Not a radical cohort of Fleydur. She would forbid it!

She contemplated Fleydur, wondering if he had foreseen this and cleverly, subtly introduced his plan as a part of a bigger plot. Her throat tightened. "I'd like to know who you are going to hire, Morgan," she said with a cough. "Surely you will not let the court children be taught by just Fleydur himself?"

Cloud-wing took the parachute, gave Dandelion the rope, and waved good-bye after their lesson. Dandelion had just managed to slide shut the window when somebird started banging on her door.

She opened it. "Olga?"

Olga was screeching, and it took a while for Dandelion to realize that she was doing so out of joy. "Guess what?" she cried to Dandelion, doing a little dance that jiggled her ankle ribbons. "Tutor Simplicio is gone. Away! My father told me that we're not having regular school until a new tutor is hired!"

Behind Olga stood two female eaglets Dandelion had

not met face-to-face before. The corners of their beaks curved coyly.

"Miss Dandelion," one of the eaglets said. "Congratulations!"

The other eaglet stepped forward and gave her a delicate hug.

Dandelion stumbled back, startled. *Did she just call me "miss"?* "What have I done?"

Even Olga was really affable. "You won!"

"Since Tutor Simplicio has left, we decided to hold our own celebration during the hour of study tomorrow," one of the eaglets explained. "Remember the paintings? Well, our class voted this morning on our favorite model during the summer term, and you won by a large margin. You even beat the queen!" It caught Dandelion unawares, but they were not finished.

"I hope our winner will accept this invitation to a masquerade tomorrow morning," the other female eaglet said, drawing from the pocket of her dress a card bedecked with bows.

"Please say you'll come, Dandelion," begged Olga. Dandelion was not sure if she felt embarrassed, shy, or dazed.

"What's a masquerade?" she said.

"A fun party where birds dress up and wear masks."

"I don't have a mask."

"You don't need one!" One of the eaglets giggled.

"Really, it doesn't matter," said the other eaglet. "Be yourself. All we want is you. And it'll be really entertaining. There'll be cake and pie."

"And caviar," added Olga.

Dandelion was at a loss for words. She saw no reason to refuse. "Yes," she said.

Try as she might that night, Dandelion could not keep her eyes shut. *Our favorite.* The words were like the smell of freshly baked bread.

Masks cannot hide the expression of eyes.
—FROM THE *BOOK OF HERESY*

11
MASQUERADE

In the morning, Fleydur asked to see Dandelion at noon in his study. She would go after the party, she decided.

As Dandelion hurried down the hall, she saw Cloud-wing.

"Are you going to the masquerade?" she asked.

Cloud-wing shook his head. "I'm visiting the old mine today with my father. He's overseeing the removal of debris to find out if the mine could be reopened." Cloud-wing paused, a troubled look in his eyes. "The masquerade . . . it won't be much fun. Don't go, Dandelion."

"But they invited me," she said. It would be rude to not show up after she had agreed.

She smoothed the folds on her garments, hoping that neatness would make up for the simplicity of her clothes and that she would not seem too out of place.

When Dandelion arrived at Simplicio's room, her beak dropped open at the scene.

Along the table, there were little silver cups almost the size of thimbles, and by each cup, a miniature spoon. There was a black gel-like substance in the cups; that must be the caviar. One eaglet picked up the tiny eating utensils and proceeded to nibble daintily at the caviar, a claw nail in the air.

But Dandelion could only gawk at the partygoers themselves. The eaglets were gesturing theatrically and chatting in singsong voices. They wore elaborate coats and gowns of silk, satin, chiffon, or velvet. One bird had such puffed sleeves they kept dipping into cups and knocking over glasses. Another's dress had layers of ruffles upon ruffles, which swept the floor like a broom when she walked. Ribbons of every color swirled from headdresses. Buttons of every size and shape gleamed in long rows.

Everybird stopped talking and looked at Dandelion. That was when she saw their masks, beautiful, beaded, feathered, and sequined. They dazzled her.

"Oh, Dandelion! It's good you came," said the creature with the sweeping ruffles. Her mask was purple and pink and silver, with bits of colored tinsel sticking out like passionflower petals.

"The party was getting dull," added another creature through his polka-dotted mask. They laughed, rustling their costumes. "Now we'll *really* have some fun!"

The creatures held Dandelion's wings and led her into the center of the room, and giggling, they twirled her around and around. Without warning, five of the caglets linked wings in a circle, with Dandelion in the center. More creatures formed a bigger ring around them, and still others made an even bigger ring enclosing them all. They swayed and ran in circles, holding wings, around her.

At first she laughed with them. It seemed to be a lighthearted little game. She tried to break out of the circles, but each time the tittering creatures jostled her back into the center.

By and by she stopped enjoying herself, and she

looked with a small frown at the twirling figures. They kept moving in on her, closing her in. She tried again to burst free, in earnest this time. Great Spirit, they were persistent. The pushing and shoving got rougher as they danced, still laughing like before.

Dandelion shoved back, not feeling playful anymore. The creatures resisted her attempts, lifted talons, and started poking and plucking her feathers. Smarting from the pain, Dandelion pushed once again. This time the creature with the passionflower mask blocked her path.

"Let go of me. Let me out!" Dandelion shouted.

Perhaps they weren't smiling as they sang and laughed. They might have never smiled. It was only their masks that made them look happy. It was only the masks that made them feel daring and strong.

She reached up, caught hold of the passionflower mask, and yanked.

She heard the string break with a snap, and then a mortified cry. Somebird abruptly tripped her. Dandelion landed hard on the floor, banging her head. What were the rules in this game they played? The rings finally broke apart; the creatures grew silent. They stopped prancing and regarded her, while their maskless companion scurried off and took cover behind them, hiding her face.

Dandelion could feel a bump rising on her head. She

let go of her trophy, trying to get up. Then the bird in the polka-dot mask bent down toward Dandelion. For a moment she thought he was aiming his crooked foot at her face, but he was merely extending talons to help her.

She stood, blinking. "Oh, Dandelion, all right, all right," said Polka-dot Mask. "We were just having fun. That's all." And the others suddenly grew friendly and cheerful as before, joining in the laughter, patting Dandelion's back. Somebird leaned down and picked up the passionflower mask, passing it back to its owner.

"Are you okay?" said Polka-dot Mask. "Are you ready for some more fun?"

"I'm so, so sorry, I didn't realize you didn't know how to play," trilled another.

"You didn't hurt your head *that* much, did you?" asked a third.

They apologized profusely, and then showered her with more well-meaning inquiries.

Why is it that when they are so polite, they seem so cruel? Dandelion thought. Her cheeks trembled and ached, and to her shock her eyes grew moist.

"We've a nifty surprise for you," Polka-dot Mask said. "No more dancing," he added.

"Come, Dandelion! Come!" the masked creatures cried, and the next moment, they crowded in and threw her onto their shoulders, securing her ankles. Carried along by the surge of the crowd, Dandelion bounced and tipped from side to side. "Set me down," she yelled, batting at the masks with her wings. Her voice was drowned out by the crowd's cheers. They crossed a threshold.

"All right," said Polka-dot Mask. Dandelion jumped off at the first opportunity and glanced around. She was standing in a gallery of canvases. Paintings of her, from Simplicio's class days ago. Only something was terribly wrong about each and every painting, terribly wrong with the whole masquerade. *"Our favorite,"* they had said. They did not mean it, not at all. She looked over her shoulder. They were standing there, anticipating her reaction, waiting for the thrilling finale they had so painstakingly planned.

So many sequined faces, staring at her, with angelic expressions glued on.

Somebird said something. She did not catch what was said. She just blocked it out, kept her face stony. And the laughter that followed? She didn't know why they laughed, but it was the ugliest sound she'd ever heard.

"Leave me alone!" she shouted.

They slipped away behind her, leaving her to face all those grotesque images of herself. In one she resembled a dung pile with a mold-colored beak. In another she was drooling and had fleas. *A foolish, clumsy, dirty bird, a bumpkin here for entertainment,* those canvases whispered to her. She wanted to push down the easels. Angry tears welled in her eyes. And they'd had the nerve to invite her to a party in her honor! She sent the wooden easels toppling, but her satisfaction gave way to a more acute pain, because she was not hurting the other eaglets by destroying their canvases. The irony made her blood boil inside.

A few paintings remained. Dandelion stared at them, fuming, but she noticed that the one in the back looked different. In that painting she looked like a normal eaglet, her wings wide open against a background of sky. "Cloud-wing's," she murmured, and she was right. She saw how with a few strokes of the brush, he'd made her look suspended in the breeze. Gazing at his painting, she felt he was sending a secret message to her: Fly now.

Dandelion dashed back to her room. She would not stay here any longer.

She sorted through the neatly piled dresses and robes, chose the ones she would need the most, carefully placing them into a towel. Then she added bits of bread she'd saved for a journey like this. And finally the braided leather rope with which Cloud-wing had taught her to fly. She tied the corners of the towel together, lifted the bundle, and approached the window.

But wait. She wouldn't take any of it, she realized suddenly. She dropped the towel and opened it again, looking at its contents. The lacy dresses of the elite weren't hers. She removed Cloud-wing's rope and hesitated. But now it made no difference whether she had it or not. This was the flight that she was going to do all alone. No other bird would be holding on to the rope; she would rely on her own strength.

With just a candle she had come; with just a candle she would leave. She checked to make sure it was still in her pocket, and left everything else behind. Turning her back to the hypocrisy and arrogance of the mountaintop, she opened the window, took a deep breath, and jumped.

Home is a nest of sweet dreams.
—FROM THE OLD SCRIPTURE

12
THE FLIGHT HOME

I *want my home! I want my family! I want to be loved*
and be happy, thought Dandelion.

The wind pulled at the feathers on her cheeks,
and she opened her wings, feeling them catch the lift.
Her muscles strained, and her bones felt brittle, like
glass, but she wouldn't fall this time. No matter how
long the journey was, she would make it home.

As Dandelion opened her eyes wide, the ring of

mountain peaks around Sword Mountain resembled a gathering of hunched eagles raising their wings so they met in a triangle high above their backs. Waiting to take flight.

Yet even if every peak in the range soared high, Dandelion would still plunge down to where her heavy heart would pull her. She let herself glide lower and lower. The sensation felt familiar, as if she had flown back this way too many times. She strained her eyes, but her vision had already begun to blur.

Mama. Papa. I'm coming home. It will be just like before.

She opened all her senses to catch any murmur of reply. But the valley only brought her the scent of weeping rain—the rich sweetness of damp acorns on the ground, tucked under layers of waxy leaves; the smell of crisp white roots of clover; the fragrance of pine resin kissed by mist again. It was like the steam of freshly brewed tea, but it choked her instead of comforting her.

Dandelion compromised: *I don't need to see you, I don't need to hear you. I just need to feel your presence. The balm of your smiles. The warmth of your wings.*

Only the orange fungi ears of fallen logs listened to her. In reply, wagging tongues of ivy leaves clattered softly against one another in the breeze.

I tried my best! Dandelion said in her mind. Her eyes closed, and she hurled herself down the tree-lined slopes. She landed clumsily on the top of the cliff, and for a moment could only huddle there. *Am I still your little Dandelion?*

Dandelion picked herself up and stumbled, digging her talons into the soft wax of her candle. There was a small hut built into a cave. There was her grand castle. She swallowed and edged forward. What did she want to see?

Dandelion stepped inside, her eyes closed. "I'm here," she said. She sat down. In the monstrous silence she felt two hearts beating in time with her own. She held on to her candle and concentrated on their steady thumps, delighted to find that they grew clearer, louder, and more substantial. She was sure that one heart was her father's as he sat scraping skins, holding his blunt bone knife, next to the fireplace, and the other was her mother's, who was sitting across from him, content, weaving on a loom.

It was reality for a heart-wrenching second. Dandelion so wanted to touch her parents she leaped up and opened her eyes.

The vision blew away.

Tears dripped from Dandelion's face, making small

dark furrows in the thick dust on the floor.

She got up waveringly and went outside. Without thinking, she spread her wings wide and glided down. Below her there was a space beneath a tree, marked with a ring of pebbles. Graves—how could she not have noticed them before? The memory of the archaeopteryx once again possessed her mind, but this time it flowed unchecked. The archaeopteryx leaping toward her, talons slashing. Her mother, furious, jumping upon the enemy; then both of them tumbling into the air. . . . Her father screaming in agony as her mother crashed to the forest floor. . . . Her father fighting maniacally, weaponless, against the archaeopteryx. . . . Dandelion leaping down, and in her fall, she already knew. . . .

She had always known.

Dandelion landed by the graves of her parents. "Mama!" she whispered. "Mama, I can fly now. I found my strength: I flew to find you."

Emptied by grief, Dandelion lay unmoving till nightfall, when she returned to the cave and curled up on the hearth of her old home. Frost was everywhere; winter was coming. A chill was setting in Dandelion's heart as she breathed shallowly, clutching her cold candle and looking at the empty blackness of the hearth.

"Dandelion!"

Dandelion hadn't heard anybird come in, but Fleydur stood behind her now, stooping over.

"Why do you think I am called Dandelion?" she shouted. "I have no place anywhere. I am unwanted. I am a weed."

"Never. Never that," said Fleydur quietly. He took a handkerchief, reached out, and gently wiped at Dandelion's eyes. "Listen to me. A dandelion is bright and noble, just like the sun. It's not haughty like a rose, not flamboyant like a jasmine, not feeble like a lily. Simple and resilient and wild," he whispered. "Unlike the garden flowers, it calls no attention to itself, demands no care from others—it can depend on itself. Maybe it's not tall or big, but it can live, and thrive, in a crack of stone, trampled and uprooted, through drought and flood alike. Because it has inner strength. It has character. Underappreciated, but it is the best of flowers."

Fleydur paused. "I am sorry that I hid from you the truth about your parents. I was waiting for the right moment to tell you. I wanted to be sure you were strong enough."

"I know," said Dandelion.

"What are you going to do now? The court agreed to let me begin my music lessons. Would you like to be one of my students?"

"I'm not sure if the eaglets will accept me," said Dandelion. "Nobird from the valley goes to school on the summit."

"There's nothing wrong with being a valley bird at all. It doesn't matter," said Fleydur. "The summit can be your home as well. And you can be my daughter."

Dandelion was stunned.

"How can I?" she said. "What about you? The court, the Iron Nest? The traditions?" Her gratitude was tempered by the gravity of what his offer meant and what it might bring.

"Don't worry so much," said Fleydur. "The Iron Nest can't do a thing; this is a personal choice. The title of princess will protect you. I can't bear to leave you here, Dandelion. You're not well yet!"

"My wounds have scarred over already." Dandelion pointed to her shoulders.

Fleydur traced the raised ridges beneath her feathers, and his eyes grew wet. "Physical injuries can mend in a guesthouse. But emotional hurts only heal in a home."

He extended a wing. "Dandelion, will you come back?" asked Fleydur. "Will you make a new home with me?"

She cried.

"To fly well, you have to fall first." She had fallen. But

with Fleydur's help, she must pick herself up again. The rough wind was not over. *Fleydur doesn't really know what the mountaintop is like*, Dandelion thought. Maybe he'd been away too long; maybe he had never really known. But she did. She knew that the queen disliked Fleydur, and knew that eagles like Simplicio hated the idea of any change. She knew there were dangers Fleydur himself did not see. She would have to return. Not for herself, but for him. Once he had saved her life, and now she needed to look out for him.

As the orange dawn burnished the edges of the mountain, Dandelion realized that she no longer wanted to hide and be a peasant. With a pounding heart, she accepted the responsibilities of a princess.

Flattery can make even a statue smile.
—FROM THE *BOOK OF HERESY*

13
ON THE MAKING OF A TUTOR

We need to hire a new tutor for the castle eaglets," said the king.

"Who?" cried Sigrid.

"Somebird new."

"Who?"

"Somebird intelligent."

"Who?"

"Somebird innovative," said Morgan. "Now please,

dear, you're sounding like an owl. I can't name the bird right this second."

The queen's beak trembled. "It matters very much to me, Morgan," she said. "I do not know what Fleydur is up to—but the eaglets should study other subjects besides music. I must make sure of it. I will find the right bird myself."

In the silence of evening, a hooded figure emerged from the shadows and glided toward a piece of parchment nailed to a tree. After reading it, he reached out and took it down, rolled it up, stuck it inside his garment, and vanished.

Kawaka was nearly bursting with delight. Making sure nobird had followed him, he returned to Tranglarhad's lair behind the waterfall.

Inside, the owl was bent over tinted eyeglass lenses. "Either the glass is too opaque, or there are too many trapped bubbles in it!" Tranglarhad grumbled to himself. The ultimate pair of sunglasses eluded him, and with it, the dreams of a nocturnal bird hoping to blend into a diurnal majority. He stopped his work at the sound of Kawaka's voice: "The opportunity has come." The archaeopteryx handed over the paper.

Tranglarhad's eyes shifted left to right, left to right.

"Tutor! The Castle of Sky wishes to procure a tutor, with substantial age and experience, to be also a member of the Iron Nest. . . ." Tranglarhad paused. "Hmm . . . minimal lodging provided within the castle; pay is three-fourths of a coin per week, maximum, nonnegotiable . . . interviews to be held tomorrow." Tranglarhad looked hard at Kawaka.

Kawaka stared back, smirking.

"You mean me?" Tranglarhad blinked, pointing to himself.

"Naturally." Kawaka nodded.

The owl considered his tattered figure.

"Aren't you a master of disguise?" the archaeopteryx demanded.

There was a pause. "What about my dignity?" said the owl.

"There's everything to gain, to learn, to find!" added the archaeopteryx.

And Tranglarhad stroked the bristles around his beak and murmured, "True, true. Children are the easiest to extract information from. And teaching is a good alibi. Draws the least suspicion."

"Nobird will deny that an owl is wise," said the archaeopteryx. "And wouldn't it be nice to be somebird important among creatures of the day?"

"True, true," said the owl once more. "I'll need an unstylish suit, some spectacles, I expect. . . . Something is still missing." Tranglarhad paced restlessly. "A weapon for the job," he muttered.

"A crossbow? An assassin's blade?"

The owl laughed. "Holy hoot, no! I need," said he, "a textbook." Tranglarhad turned to Kawaka, reaching out a talon. "Give me the *Book of Heresy*!"

"What?" Kawaka leaped aside, hugging the book to his chest. "This is the life work of my emperor."

Tranglarhad snatched again. "Only that book will do! Do you or don't you want me to succeed in stealing the Leasorn gem from the eagles? I am risking a lot if I go to assume this paltry post of tutor and leave my mine to my underlings." The owl glowered. "You, you who started our pact, are you not willing to make an equal sacrifice?"

Kawaka unclenched his talons and slowly handed the leatherbound book to the owl. "The moment you return, you give it back to me!" he growled.

Pleased, Tranglarhad left to prepare.

He unearthed an antiquated coat and shook its folds heartily, sending forth a moldy cloud of dust. As the initial odor cleared, he sprayed cheap cologne that only made it smell worse. Then he draped his attire over a stalagmite and crept to an underground pool for a bath. Tranglarhad did not recall ever having a bath in his life. *I must rise—rinse—to the occasion,* he thought, and dipped himself in. His feathers were a drastic shade lighter when he climbed out. As his plumage dried, Tranglarhad used a pair of tiny silver scissors to trim his bristles. He perched a pair of thick round spectacles upon his beak and looked at his reflection in a pool. *Suave and debonair, as usual,* he thought.

Satisfied, Tranglarhad put on the old coat and tied on the tackiest bow tie in his possession. He swept several other unfashionable outfits and a gift-wrapped package into a suitcase. "Ah! I almost forgot," he muttered, and rummaged through his alchemist's potions to produce a vial containing a single golden pill. This too went into the suitcase. Finally, Tranglarhad surprised Kawaka by packing a bottle of peanut oil and a small black cauldron.

"What are those for?" asked the archaeopteryx.

"I have my reasons," huffed the owl. At length he stood up and tucked the *Book of Heresy* into the pocket of his coat.

"Good luck," said Kawaka.

"Luck? I don't need any." The owl laughed. And on silent wings, he emerged from the bowels of the mountain and headed for its summit.

News spread through Skythunder mountain range so that before dawn, dozens of applicants were camped outside the castle waiting for their interviews. A spot in the Iron Nest! With all the bragging rights and privileges attached, it was a true once-in-a-lifetime opportunity.

At noon, the hopefuls were allowed inside. The birds that strutted in with beaks overflowing with verse and poetry stumbled out again within minutes, their feathers quivering and their faces mournful. The line was fast dwindling, but as evening fell, a latecomer appeared. The last applicant sat on his suitcase by his cauldron and waited calmly.

"All right. Your turn!" shouted a guard.

The applicant sauntered in, ready to combat the chilling gaze of an austere bird who sat in judgment.

Queen Sigrid was slumped on her couch, a foot stuck out on a cushion for a pedicure. The applicant blinked with relief. He noted the hummingbird filing the nails on the queen's toes and repainting them cherry red, and he knew the right words to say.

"Elegant choice of color, my queen! An educated, sophisticated choice."

Sigrid preened at the flattery. *Nobird has said anything so exciting today,* she thought. She twitched her burly toes, but the applicant knew she was only waiting for more.

"Mature, stately, befitting a queen as yourself, yet with a subtle hint of youth."

"Youth . . . quite." Sigrid looked up from examining a red nail. "I am quite young! But my eyes are failing me. . . ."

"Then allow me to present an example of my handiwork, Your Majesty," said the applicant, opening his suitcase and drawing forth a package. "It's the most exquisite, queenly type of spectacles, the lorgnette."

Sigrid tore off the paper with unladylike zeal and gave a cry of delight. She held up a pair of gold-edged glasses to her eyes. Her beak hung slack. "An owl!" Sigrid nearly fell back on her couch. "And I thought you were an eagle with a big head," she said. "You realize there has never been an . . . owl among our castle staff?"

"Then I shall be honored if I am lucky enough to be the first," said Tranglarhad.

Sigrid peered at him through her new glasses. "I don't recall you telling me your name."

"I am called Tranglarhad, Your Majesty."

The queen shook her head. "Ridiculous. Your name does not sound intellectual enough for you to be qualified to teach here."

"But, Your Majesty, it's an owl name meaning 'one who has a triangular head,'" the owl cried, gesticulating at his face, pointing out three angles made by his ear tufts and his beak. "The triangle is the most stable shape in the geometric world. To have a head shaped thus is to have knowledge most securely stored within the skull!"

The queen considered, looking at her painted nails for a moment. "All right, then: What makes you think you're qualified?"

Tranglarhad knew how to answer this question. "First and foremost, I am not from the valley," he said. "I am a native of Sword Mountain, in fact. I look up to the Castle of Sky every day."

"Good."

"Second, I possess a unique book called the *Book of Heresy*," said Tranglarhad. "Allow me to share with you a passage?"

Sigrid nodded.

Tranglarhad began. "Page 249: 'Nothing will come of waiting alone. The best tacticians meticulously set multiple traps, all the while appearing quite friendly to their foes. Fatten up your enemies with your kindness, make them vulnerable so you can savor their demise. . . .'"

Sigrid was mesmerized.

"My! I do believe you to be a fine candidate," she said. "However . . ." Queen Sigrid frowned.

"What is it, my queen?" Tranglarhad murmured.

"You are a stranger. Not an eagle, and not of our tribe. The post of tutor, as you know, allows you a vote in the Iron Nest. It's against the customs to allow a stranger into our government." Sigrid looked torn. "I would still like to hire you, only as a tutor," she said slowly. "I simply cannot give you a position in the Iron Nest assembly."

"I would be honored to be a plain tutor," said Tranglarhad.

"Then it is settled," said Sigrid. "Will you be fit to teach tomorrow morning?"

"Will evening do?" asked the owl. "I am nocturnal."

Sigrid nodded, beginning to trust the owl. "Evening classes shall be fine. Though you may see if the physician can prescribe medications for your ailment; being nocturnal is an unfortunate handicap. And after your classes, will you come to my drawing room to read me your philosophy book? I like it very much."

"It shall be my pleasure, Your Majesty," said the owl.

A handicap? he thought. *Queen Sigrid, you are much in the dark.*

Music is laughter in radiant feathers.
—FROM THE OLD SCRIPTURE

14

A LEGITIMATE SCANDAL

Dandelion was staring at a door that hid something she did not want to face.

"As a princess, you must formally greet and acknowledge the subjects of your generation, the children of the court. They've just been gathered a minute ago, waiting inside. They've been told they have a new princess, but they do not know who yet. You must greet them, show them who you are," Fleydur was saying.

The door's varnished panel reflected six glints in her image: her crown and the five gold acorns pinned on her collar. But there was neither window nor crack in the door to let her peek at the other side. "Greet them!" Dandelion said. *But they . . . they hate me. And I hate them.*

"Just as the king heads and cares for the court, so as a princess you must assume the leadership of the younger birds of Sword Mountain," said Fleydur. "You have special responsibility—you must learn to love them, Dandelion." He walked away, leaving Dandelion alone.

A lump rose in Dandelion's throat. She could not love these eaglets. But she swallowed and made herself turn the doorknob and step in, shutting the door behind her.

The eaglets stood up, faces expressionless. They were dressed in ceremonial suits and dresses. So dizzyingly different from the last time she had seen them gathered together, snickering behind extravagant masks.

Dandelion approached them. "Hello," she said.

For a moment, the eaglets seemed too stunned to remember their voices. "Hello," they echoed, waiting. Cloud-wing smiled. Olga looked dismayed. Pudding eyed Dandelion. "The masquerade wasn't enough for you? Do you want more?" he seemed to say.

She felt a sudden rush of defiant calm. "I chose to come back," she told them. "I want to be friends with you." Dandelion turned to Pudding and thrust her talons toward him, ready to parry malice with courtesy.

After a pause, Pudding shook her claws, his meaty grip crushing her talons till tears sprang in her eyes. She stood firm, and she shook talons with them all, one by one.

Though parents objected to Fleydur's radical teaching, nobird could hold back the children from missing out on a potentially juicy scandal.

When Fleydur announced that he would hold his music lessons on the very top of Sword Mountain, every member of the class was present and, in fact, early, waiting near the base of Sword Cliff.

And so were the eight members of the Iron Nest who had, along with Simplicio, opposed Fleydur. Since it was hard to be inconspicuous among the barren piles of rock, they gave up trying to pretend they had just happened to be there and hunched matter-of-factly in a half circle around the children.

Their rheumy eyes glinted suspiciously, and their faces were grim; each held a notepad, leaning forward, posed to scribble atrocities. "You won't mind, prince, our monitoring your lesson?" thundered one. "As the Iron Nest, it is our firm duty to control and guard the egg of Sword Mountain's future."

Fleydur swept his wing in a gesture of welcome. "Delighted."

As for Dandelion herself, she was looking at Fleydur intently. She thought he was nervous and feared that he would say something rash. The members of the Iron Nest were only too ready to misinterpret if not outright twist his lessons in their notes.

But Fleydur started from the beginning and taught them the notes and the names of the scale. The children chanted the unfamiliar syllables: "*Do, re, mi, fa, so, la, ti, do!*"

"Very good, very good!" said Fleydur. "Now sing loudly; don't be afraid, there's hardly anybird to hear you, other than the Iron Nest. Call out in a clear, loud voice—try to match the sound of my trumpet!" Fleydur brought his silver trumpet to his beak and blew slowly, a note at a time, a lively, simple tune.

"Olga?" said Fleydur. "Why are you not singing?"

Olga fidgeted, and she did not open her beak for some time. "I'm just worried, Prince Fleydur," she said. "I remembered that you can't open your beak wider than thirty degrees!" Olga was acutely distressed. "It's in the *Handbook of the Feathered Aristocrat*."

"You read that thing?" said Pouldington, tugging at his collar, so that the four fat gold acorn pins there clacked against one another. Olga ducked her head, more uncomfortable than before, aware of her half acorn.

"You remember. 'A refined eagle should at all times position the two mandibles of his or her beak at no greater than a thirty-degree angle.'" Olga tilted her head and gravely turned her profile to the group to demonstrate. "Twenty degrees for eating everything except caviar, for which twenty-five is permitted."

"But your voice is truly beautiful, Olga," said Fleydur. "You should open your beak wide and sing."

At this, Olga burst into tears.

"The prince harshly coerces a well-bred young lady, who is versed in the fine literature of our traditions, to 'sing,' against her wishes!" whispered an old scholar to a colleague.

Fleydur looked very concerned. "Olga? Are you all right?"

Olga nodded through her tears. "Yes. Nobird . . . nobird has ever told me that I am beautiful!"

She sang the tune again, exactly as Fleydur had played upon his trumpet. Though her talking voice was deep and hoarse, when she sang, it was a surprisingly sweet soprano. Her song lingered, echoing faintly in the valleys all around.

All the children flapped their wings furiously in applause, and Fleydur clapped the hardest of all. The eight members of the Iron Nest frowned at one another.

"Tell me, Prince," demanded one of the scholars. "What significance has this fooling around?"

"Why, sir, can't you see how happy music can make us?" exclaimed Fleydur. "Music can brighten our lives every day. It's all around us!"

"Even in the Castle of Sky?" Olga exclaimed.

Fleydur's eyes twinkled. "I'll show you. Class, we'll have a music tour!"

Wiggling with anticipation and curiosity, the eaglets leaped up from the boulders and followed Fleydur back down to the castle. Fleydur fished drumsticks out of his pockets, which he twirled as he flew.

On the metal gates, the wooden doors, the glass windows he beat as he hummed a tune. Down the Hall of Mirrors he gently tapped his reflections, one after another. In the castle kitchens he swept past the cooks, drumming a hearty symphony on the pots and pans. He tapped the glass pitchers filled with water, appreciating their lingering pure notes.

"What, my prince, what are you doing?" demanded the chef. "This is a serious job, the feeding of a whole castle of dignitaries!" However, soon he laughed and joined in, banging a soup cauldron; the undercooks, too, rattled forks and spoons together.

"I bet you can't make music from this!" Pudding challenged Fleydur, grabbing a carrot from a basket.

Fleydur examined the carrot carefully, then, borrowing a knife from the chef, hollowed it out and carved holes along its length. He lifted the carrot to his beak and blew a silly tune.

Everybird laughed as Pudding squealed in astonishment. When Fleydur handed the carrot to him, he huffed and puffed and could only make sputtering sounds. Shrugging, Pudding crunched the carrot in his beak and ate it instead.

"Did you see that? The prince even crusades against table manners," a member of the Iron Nest observed to another.

Fleydur picked up two lids and clapped them together like cymbals before he led his class toward the audience chamber. Castle staff trailed after the troop of delighted eaglets, gawking at the sight of the Iron Nest shuffling along involuntarily in the parade.

The bronze statue with the scales stood alone in the

chamber. Playfully Fleydur struck the scales, and in the sonorous note that followed, the bronze eagle swayed side to side as if in appreciation.

Dandelion felt relieved. She'd been preparing to defend Fleydur from the court children. Was it because she didn't understand these eaglets, or because the music had made them act differently? She wanted to experience more of the music to find out. "What song are you humming?" asked Dandelion. "Can you teach it to us?"

Fleydur laughed and said, "Only if you sing along with me as we go!"

The eaglets obliged. As Fleydur lead them farther into the castle, toward the treasury, they were soon singing:

What is joy?
Flying kites together, sprinkles on a cake
Spiraling up high to meet the first snowflake
Tag around a tree, stories on the hearth
Dancing after school, laughter full of mirth
Soaring in the sky, up where you belong
Eating lots of pies, singing lots of songs.
The best joy is certain: being on Sword Mountain.

They were stopped, however, at the treasury, by four birds in uniform armed with lances.

"Stop, Prince! You cannot sing here!" shouted one of the treasury guards.

"But King Morgan has allowed music, hasn't he?" said Fleydur, surprised. Their singing trailed off.

The treasury guard acknowledged it with a nod but was firm. "There is one exception, explicitly written. You cannot sing within ten paces of the treasury."

Fleydur was surprised, but he did not step back. "All right, I shall enter without singing," he said.

Yet at his first step forward, the guards blocked his path with their lances. "I'm sorry. Recently the queen told us that nobird can enter the treasury without her or the king's permission."

"I do not want to take anything out; I just want to show my students one thing," said Fleydur.

All four guards frowned. "And we were given orders by the queen to be especially cautious about that one thing."

Seeing that it was impossible to go past, Fleydur turned around and led his students back out of the castle to the base of Sword Cliff, tearing off leaves and making whistles from them along the way.

As they settled on their boulders again, Pouldington, more familiar with the treasury than any other eaglet, asked, "What one thing, Fleydur? I mean, the gold coins made nice clinking sounds, but what is so special that you kept it for last on our music tour?"

Fleydur paused for a moment. "Have you heard of the Leasorn gemstone?"

Some of the older and higher-ranked eaglets gasped, but most had no clue.

"My father says it's a beautiful purple stone that gives off light!" said Pudding.

"So it is, but it is much more," said Fleydur. "All of the six Leasorn gems can glow, but each has a unique property; for instance, the green Leasorn of the parrots can heal. And ours? Ours is a singing gemstone." He paused. "A singing gemstone in a place devoid of song," Fleydur whispered.

"What makes it sing?" asked Dandelion.

"It would only sing when you approach it with a strong emotion that cannot be adequately expressed in words," said Fleydur. "When you say to the Leasorn, 'Sing my heart,' it transforms your emotion into melody. Back when it wasn't guarded so closely, I listened to its tunes. But when Queen Sigrid discovered its secret, she locked it deep in the treasury for safekeeping, within soundproof walls. Few really know of its power."

"But why?" Pudding asked.

"I suppose emotions can seem . . . dangerous.

Sometimes we don't understand them, and ignore them. Yet they are an important part of who we are. They give us insight and make us reflect and think."

Perhaps the queen is afraid of what birds might hear, Dandelion thought. *Or how they might be changed by the music.*

Fleydur sighed, remembering. "And the song of joy that we sang together was the first song the Leasorn sang to me."

"Will we ever hear its music?" asked Olga.

"I will try to find a way to show it to you," said Fleydur. "Somehow."

When class was over, Dandelion found herself flying beside Olga back to the castle. She looked over at Olga, wanting to say something, but Olga seemed absorbed in something else. Abruptly, Olga turned to her.

"What?"

They were at the staircase where they had collided not long ago. This time, Dandelion recalled Olga's sweet voice.

"I like your singing."

Olga blinked, then grew embarrassed. "Thanks," she said.

*You can rarely get what you really want; you can
easily get what you don't want.*
—FROM THE *BOOK OF HERESY*

15
OWL PHILOSOPHIES

Tranglarhad placed the black cap of the tutor upon his round head and felt empowered. Though the inch of office space he'd been given was windowless and cold and, he deduced from the mothball smell, once a closet, he was elated to find that he already claimed a bit of space, no matter how small, on the mountaintop. He took off his sunglasses. No candle or lamp had been provided, but he was quite at ease in the dark.

"First lesson," the owl intoned, rocking back and forth on his toes. Gathering his instruments of instruction, he crossed the hall to the classroom.

As evening grew late, eaglets began to fill the room, some grumbling, others wide-eyed at the sight of the owl. Tranglarhad noticed a princess among the students.

"Your name?" he said to her as she went by.

"I'm Dandelion," she said.

"Should we sit in the order of our status?" one eaglet asked hopefully, interrupting Tranglarhad's train of thought.

"Sit wherever you like," said Tranglarhad, turning back to the class. "You cannot hide from me."

There was a general shifting as birds crisscrossed the room. Dandelion had been sitting in the front row, a few spaces from Cloud-wing, and she stayed put so she could have a good look at the tutor. But Olga rushed forward and claimed the seat next to Dandelion. She smoothed her feathers, a permanent smile on her face, as she continually flicked her eyes toward Cloud-wing.

On the blackboard, the teacher had scrawled:

$$Mr. \Delta$$

"My name is Mr. Tranglarhad," he said. "I am your new tutor, and I have a viewpoint different from all teachers who have set talon in this castle. I do not see you in terms of rank, status, class, or gender. I see you all equal—" Tranglarhad pronounced grandly at the hopeful faces. Dandelion couldn't believe her ears at first; Olga's claw drifted to her half acorn.

"Equally stupid!" He allowed an adequate pause for the effect to sink in. "Now, as to whether this is true or not, it is up to you to show me. There shall be challenging opportunities, I'm sure."

Cloud-wing glanced at Dandelion and Olga. His expression seemed to say, "What do you think of him?" Olga blinked, bewildered, but Dandelion gave a defiant shrug.

The door flew open. Pudding huffed and puffed, leaning against the door frame, his eyes bulging in terror as he caught sight of the owl, swiveling his head a hundred and eighty degrees to glare at him.

"You know what it means to be tardy?" said Tranglarhad. Silence fell across the classroom.

"Tarty?" said Pudding. "Eating too many tarts, becoming bloated, and oversleeping?" Nervous laughter came from the eaglets; they'd never seen Pudding frightened before. He touched his four acorn pins to reassure himself of his rank. He hazarded a step toward a perch among the eaglets, but Tranglarhad cried, "Stop! Pouldington, is it? Stand here and listen. What did Simplicio do to a bird who was ten minutes late?" Tranglarhad's gaze swept over Dandelion to Olga.

Olga's frilly capped head was trembling. "One whack with a rod, but he hardly ever hit Pudding, sir!"

The owl faced the treasurer's son again. "Oh, privileges, have you? You all heard me: I believe in fairness."

Pudding's beak burst open. Even Dandelion felt awful for him as he blubbered and stumbled. High up on his podium, Tranglarhad watched placidly.

"Perhaps you are in luck," the owl said finally. "My rule number one: There shall be no traditional caning in my class." Cheers erupted from the eaglets, and Pudding breathed a sigh of relief.

Tranglarhad waved an airy set of talons. "I deem it backward, primitive, and particularly useless as it inspires—ah, shall we say?—not enough fear. No, the fear that I want to see is one that will brand your minds: true, cold fear that comes when you are not sure exactly what will befall you but know that it will be hideous."

Stunned silence.

"My punishments must therefore be singular." Tranglarhad gave another of his dramatic pauses. "But we're wasting time. Pouldington, take your seat. I will inform you of your punishment by and by."

Dandelion saw that Tranglarhad was intent on

torturing Pudding as the lessons began with mathematics.

"I have a butchering knife the shape of a right triangle," said Tranglarhad. "The knife is four inches lengthwise—perfect for disciplinary uses—and three inches wide at the base. How long is the diagonal edge of the blade?"

Everybird's wing was raised. Everybird's except Pudding's. "Pouldington? Answer the question, please."

"I . . . I . . ."

"Can you or can't you? Yes or no?"

"No. I don't understand, sir."

"But this is straightforward geometry. You have, as an aid, eight claws on your talons, and quite enough feathers on your wings to do multiplication. Give me the first step, at least. What is four squared? Think, what's four times four?"

Silence.

"This will not do," said the owl. "Unless you give a plausible reason for this shameful deficiency, Pouldington, I'm afraid this will add on to the punishment for your tardiness."

"Please, sir! My father—"

"What has your father got to do with this?"

"He's the treasurer of Sword Mountain."

"Treasurer?" Tranglarhad's eyes grew rounder. "Holy

hoot, that's a thousand times worse. If that's what he is, why in the world can you not do mathematics?"

"No, yes, I mean . . ." Pudding swallowed hard. "What I meant to say is, he isn't good at math, either!"

"What are you talking about?"

"My dad says, 'Mathematics, it adds to my temper, it subtracts from my appetite, it divides my attention, and it multiplies my workload!'" He paused as half the class laughed and the other half remained uneasily silent. "So I figured, if it was a good enough reason for him, it's good enough for me," Pudding said in a small voice, cowering.

"Oh, really," said Tranglarhad. He stared at Pouldington. "All right then. Enough math for today." He had planned to do a philosophy lesson from the *Book of Heresy*, but the information Pouldington had provided called for a change of action.

Thinking quickly, he brightened and said, "Now, an exercise in the language arts." He paced up and down the rows. "Many before me have told you, but today I demonstrate for you yet again: 'Show, don't tell.' To do so, it's helpful to have a mastery of descriptive language." Tranglarhad grabbed a stick of chalk and wrote on the blackboard:

There is a stone in the room.

He whipped his head around to scan the faces of his students.

"Elaborate upon this sentence. What stone? Of what value? Where? In what room?"

All of the eaglets opened their beaks and called out their versions of the sentence. But Tranglarhad's ear tufts caught a snippet of words that were almost too good to be true: "There is a pretty stone, in a box, in a room, in the castle. . . ." His attention centered upon the fat treasurer's son.

"Pouldington, share with the class your sentence." Tranglarhad's eyes gleamed with intense interest.

Pudding looked as if he'd been caught raiding the pantry. He gulped and repeated what he'd said.

"Go on," breathed Tranglarhad. "Use precise words, to create a picture in the listeners' minds. What color is the stone?"

"Um . . . purple?" Pudding cringed, uncomfortable and still thinking of his upcoming punishment.

"Very good! And?"

Pudding scrunched up his eyes in concentration. "There is a pretty purple precious stone in a hidden locked iron box in a storage compartment in the fully guarded treasury underneath the tall tower of the king." He cracked open an eye.

Tranglarhad was positively beaming. "Excellent! Vivid indeed."

Pouldington looked astounded that he had gained the praise of the tutor. He relaxed.

"Ah, Pouldington?" said the owl. "Stay after class. I have just stumbled upon a fitting punishment."

Never mind that all the parents of his students wielded greater power than he did. He would break precedent and request the first parent-teacher conference of Sword Mountain.

"What is it, sir?" The treasurer's broad face was all annoyance. Never before had a tutor dared to summon him, definitely not so late at night!

"Your son," began the owl.

"Yes, yes, he's quite an amazing, intelligent, polite young lad and all that."

"Actually," the owl said, "he is not doing too well." He paused. "He is doing poorly." He paused again, twirling the bristles around his beak. "In fact, he is flunking math."

The treasurer laid a heavy set of claws upon the desk.

"Now, sir," he said in a conspiring whisper. "The duties of a treasurer are numerous, and many are not related to mathematics; even so, if the son of a treasurer fails in math . . . imagine! That would reflect badly on me!"

Tranglarhad nodded and kept nodding for some time. Finally he spoke up again. "And, oh, there is another, completely separate thing, just an academic interest . . . geology, stone samples and such . . ."

"Why, yes. You want to look at one of the odd stones we have?" The treasurer gushed eagerly, relieved. "No problem! I have the keys to the treasury."

"Indeed! Among those special stones, is there a purple gemstone?"

The treasurer froze. "No," he whimpered. "Not that. I can show you anything else. . . ."

"Just a glimpse." Tranglarhad pressed on.

"I have orders, strict orders; there's an unmentionable penalty, I can't risk that!"

Tranglarhad had to tread lightly to avoid suspicion, he knew. And retreat fast. "A pity," he said. "I thought to teach students about rocks, minerals, and where they are to be found. I am an expert in that field. Do you know, sir, for instance, that the old mine in the base of Sword Mountain has iron ore of a unique grade? It's a pity that it also contains a poisonous gas that makes it impossible to retrieve that fine ore."

"Wait a second. The mine we're opening up?" said the treasurer. "You mean that stench is gas?"

"Of course," said the owl. "Mr. Treasurer, have you not calculated the profits against the danger?" He paused to gauge the effect his words had on the treasurer. *Good,* Tranglarhad thought. *He won't bother my mine anymore.* "But in any event, sir, your son . . ."

"Yes?" said the treasurer weakly.

"Your son, he's a fine boy."

"Do you really think so?" Tears of gratitude welled into the treasurer's eyes. "Oh? Thank you. Thank you for telling me that."

The next morning, the details of the parent conference had become gossip among the eaglets, and Pudding himself recounted what he knew. Dandelion, puzzled by Tranglarhad's eccentricity, went outside and waited for Fleydur's lesson to begin. She breathed the crisp air deeply. Now that she could fly, she wanted to explore the areas around the peak. She stumbled upon a slope still straggly with the last of the fall vegetation. Along its edge were dandelions, their fluffy white heads balancing in the wind.

"How do you like being a princess?" asked Cloud-wing, coming up behind her.

"The acorns are so heavy," she said. "They strain my neck! No wonder the adults all look so stiff-necked and gloomy; they had to suffer all through eaglethood."

Cloud-wing laughed. "Princess, there is always a price to pay." And he made an extravagant bow.

Dandelion grinned. "Enough of those awful bows." She waved a wing. "Really, don't call me princess. We're friends here. I'm still Dandelion."

Cloud-wing persisted. "Have you perused your daily section of the handbook?"

"Stop!" She laughed along with him. "Being a princess really feels like an act," Dandelion admitted at last. "So many formalities." She remembered Sigrid's silence when Fleydur had announced the adoption. She'd received the circlet and acorns from the king, a hug from Fleydur, and a battered copy of the *Handbook of the Feathered Aristocrat* from the queen.

"You could make the act different," said Cloud-wing. "You could change what being a princess means."

They sat back, admiring the dandelions in the midst and the vast purple mountains behind them. The wind blew, and some of the seeds drifted off, toward peaks farther away.

"I wonder where they're going," said Dandelion.

"I bet to Rockbottom," said Cloud-wing. "Look—the

mountain with double peaks? That's where Rock-bottom is."

"How far they will have to fly?" said Dandelion.

"It's a vast stretch," answered Cloud-wing.

"And mountains in the way . . . ," she said.

"They will get there," said Cloud-wing.

At the sound of Fleydur's trumpet, they headed to their music lesson.

That day, Fleydur taught Dandelion and the rest of the eaglets how to dance the schwa-schwa, a dance widespread among birds in the forests beyond the mountain range. "Row your wings forward, flip your wings back. Clap your claws!" sang Fleydur.

They flew in loops, all the while pedaling their feet. They clapped and did a full-body feather shake. Then they dived and swooped back and forth in the air like pendulums.

The swarm of little figures going around and around Sword Cliff became an instant attraction to birds on the surrounding peaks. Telescopes pinpointed their every move.

Even the king was affected. Up in his tower, Morgan closed his eyes and swayed in a faint imitation of the dance. A wide grin spread on his old face. Deciding to delay his meeting with the Iron Nest for a minute more, he leaned his scepter against the wall, set his crown aside on the table, and started dancing as furiously as he could.

"The king is late," noted a scholar a few rooms away. Music floated into the Iron Nest as well. Two of the advisers suddenly bent their knees and bobbed in place to the tune, but just as quickly, the stern gaze of the rest centered upon them. "Sorry," the two mumbled. Straightening, they resumed the displeased looks of academics.

Sigrid was suffering in her drawing room. Even with the window shut, the curtain drawn, she found herself twitching the toes of her left foot to the rhythm. The music rang on in her head, and she thought the branch outside her window seemed to tap the pane in time. "I will have that branch cut," she shouted. "No, the tree uprooted!" Her anger pounded in her ears—even her heart was beating to the song's two-beat rhythm!

When she stormed into the gathering of the Iron Nest, one of the birds there even had the audacity to comment on the cursed music.

"Your Majesty," said the courtier in a dreamy, breathy voice, "does it not make you feel . . . young?"

"I am young," Sigrid corrected grimly.

With her glaring eye upon them, nobird in the Iron

Nest dared tap a talon or twitch a feather in time to the music.

It's as if the whole castle is drunk, Sigrid thought, sickened. *Yet these giddy eagles can hardly curb the pouring of more music.*

"What will we do for the king's birthday?" Pudding asked Fleydur once they finished dancing.

"Me?" said Fleydur. "I am not going to decide. I'll teach you songs and dances and how to play simple notes on instruments, but you'll decide what you want to show the king."

"Let's get started!" exclaimed Olga.

Fleydur led them to his tower and opened a room. "Find your instrument," he said.

It was a treasure trove. Brass instruments with their bell-shaped ends shone in open cases. Woodwinds, in order of increasing size, lined the walls. Books and sheets of music lay in neat piles.

Olga, who worried that she'd sing off-pitch even though everybird assured her otherwise, found tuning forks. Cloud-wing selected an elegant black-and-silver oboe. Pudding yelped when he tripped over a drum. "If the carrot wouldn't play for me, this surely will!" he said, and with the back of his talons slapped its skin.

Dandelion touched this instrument and tried that one. Everybird had found something special and was tinkering with it, whispering to the others excitedly or asking Fleydur how to play what he or she had found. Everybird but her.

And then she stumbled upon the blank music sheets.

Dandelion picked them up carefully. She peered at the five black lines, and they seemed to her like empty perches waiting for flocks of notes to flutter upon them.

She looked up and cried, "Let's compose our own song for the king!"

All the other eaglets looked at her, amazed at the idea.

"How?" Pouldington said awkwardly, addressing Dandelion directly for the first time since her return.

"And what will it be about?" said another eaglet.

They drifted over. "Well . . . ," Dandelion began explaining. They leaned in a circle over the music sheet. More eaglets surrounded them, all listening, their heads bent together.

The door to Fleydur's room banged open. Every eaglet turned from the music sheets to stare at the stranger who stood in the doorway.

"Look at his uniform!" Cloud-wing whispered to Dandelion. "He's from Rockbottom Academy—he must be the admissions officer."

The officer didn't even acknowledge Fleydur or explain his presence. He flipped open a ledger and began to read off a list of names—the birds who had passed their examinations. Instruments lay forgotten in their talons.

Cloud-wing's beak dropped open as he heard his name. A few around him leaped up and tussled one another in their celebration, but Cloud-wing sat still, beaming. Dandelion watched it all, more curious than ever.

The boys pumped their wings into the air and mimicked the whistling sound of an object falling in a long arc: "*Wheeeeee.* Ka-boom!" they shouted. It was the chant of the Rockbottom Academy.

"That's right, sirs!" said the admissions officer. "We are going to take you softies apart, pound you to bits, and rebuild new eagles up from the rock bottom!"

Chubby Pouldington did not get into the academy, but he didn't care. In fact, he looked relieved.

Fleydur declared the lesson over, and the eaglets left together, still excitedly discussing the acceptances to Rockbottom Academy and Dandelion's idea. Most took their new instruments with them, but Cloud-wing, after an anguished deliberation, returned it to Fleydur, as did several other Rockbottom students.

"You've been to Rockbottom for a school visit. What's it like?" Dandelion asked Cloud-wing eagerly as they flew down the staircase outside Fleydur's door. "It is really that tough?"

Cloud-wing grinned. "We're not allowed to leave the school for the first year. Every day is grueling. There are hardly any fires, and the water's freezing. In the winter months, to take a bath, you jump into a snowdrift and use a hunk of ice to scour the scales of your legs like it's a pumice stone."

"Ouch!" Dandelion said. They had arrived at the courtyard, where Dandelion had seen him practicing martial arts before.

"Aye, it's a torture institution," said Cloud-wing solemnly as he walked over to collect his armor and equipment. "The walls are granite, and the perches in the dormitory are steel bars set in little alcoves in the wall. The cook there, he's a murderous fellow! Peels potatoes with a sword. And the guards are notorious; they're not there to keep trespassers out. They are there to keep us in."

Cloud-wing drew out his claymore. "No singing. No painting anymore. No laughing, I expect." As he gazed at his reflection in the burnished blade, his voice changed.

"But when I return, when I come out, I'll be a warrior!"

Cloud-wing pranced across the courtyard, brandishing his claymore.

Dandelion felt a pang of sorrow and envy. Life at Rockbottom seemed like a series of secret rites and rituals. She had a gold circlet on her head and gold acorns on her collar, but the gold seemed dull compared with that flashing steel.

"When are you leaving?" she asked.

"Tomorrow."

Dandelion gasped. Cloud-wing stopped, sheathed his claymore, and turned back to her a little breathless. He lowered his eyes.

"I'll be plunged into a new place. Like you when you first came," he said. "All the things I'm used to, so many birds I know . . . gone. A different mountain, a different world."

"But you'll keep on being Cloud-wing," said Dandelion.

"Like you will always be Dandelion," he said.

"Good luck, Cloud-wing," she whispered, unable to say the word good-bye.

"Thanks," he said. He paused, looking at the ground. "I'll write letters. Tell you all the news. And you are a warrior, too. A different sort of warrior."

She gazed at the hazy mountaintops in the distance, at the slopes of Sword Mountain below, and held her candle tightly.

Dandelion would stay here, a warrior against those eight of the Iron Nest who opposed Fleydur and everything he stood for. She would be strong, even with Cloud-wing gone.

And the lazy bird said to the old witch, "Give me a
magic potion to cure my bad memory!"
"Why, when physical punishment will work like a
charm?" She laughed. "Indeed, indeed!"
—FROM A STORY IN THE *BOOK OF HERESY*

16
PACKAGES OF TROUBLE

"Fleydur," Dandelion said a few days later, after a music lesson, "is there a martial arts school like Rockbottom where a girl like me can attend?"

Fleydur shook his head. "Why, Dandelion?"

"I want to be able to defend myself and those I love," Dandelion said, thinking of the scars from her healed archaeopteryx wounds. Though hidden from sight beneath her feathers, they ached in the night sometimes and intensified her nightmares. "The moment I first saw Cloud-wing and his friends practicing swords, I was fascinated. I wouldn't be helpless if I learned to wield a sword, would I?" she said, and she touched the candle that she always carried in her pocket. She closed her eyes for a moment and remembered her mother and father in their little cave.

"I can teach you, Dandelion," Fleydur said.

"Really, Fleydur?"

Fleydur looked off in the distance. He was very still. "I believe I may have the right sword for you."

He led Dandelion back to the castle, where he retrieved a parcel wrapped in leather from his room. Inside was a very plain sword. The blade was webbed with scratches and chipped in one place; the hilt was stained dark with the imprint of a clenching claw. But Dandelion saw the strength of the steel, the sturdiness of the hilt, and the keen edge of the blade. Though it was well worn, it was ready to be used for years to come. Dandelion's eyes widened in delight.

"Go on, hold it," said Fleydur, excited as well.

Dandelion grasped the hilt, wrapping her talons around the clawprint. She lifted the blade in the air.

"Sweep the sword down like this." Fleydur made a motion. "That will block an opponent's blow." Frowning with concentration, Dandelion tried to mimic Fleydur's movements, and Fleydur nodded in approval.

"It's so different from the swords Cloud-wing and the others have," said Dandelion. "Where is it from?"

"It's the original sword of Wind-voice, the hero also known as Swordbird," Fleydur said. "I traveled with him. At the end of the archaeopteryx war, when Wind-voice earned the Hero's Sword, he said to me, 'I no longer have a use for this blade. It's a common but reliable sword, nothing special to a stranger, but priceless to the right bird. I entrust it to your care.' So now, Dandelion, I give it to you."

Dandelion held the sword reverently. "Thank you, Fleydur!"

Since tradition frowned upon girls learning to become warriors, and since Sigrid frowned upon Fleydur and Dandelion, they went down to the valley to train in the weeks that followed, where Sigrid could not see.

"Carry these stones up that cliff," said Fleydur on the first day. "It's important that you grow strong enough that holding the extra weight of a sword won't affect your flight."

That evening, sore all over, Dandelion was greeted by a falcon courier delivering a short letter from Cloud-wing. It read:

Dandelion,

How are you? After a hard day at Rockbottom, I can't sleep because everybird's snoring in the dormitory— and it's far from musical. Missing Sword Mountain already.

Cloud-wing

She wrote back:

Cloud-wing,

We miss you, too. Fleydur's agreed to teach me how to wield a sword! Learning swordplay is harder than flying! When I returned to the castle, Olga told me I looked as if I'd been tripping over ankle ribbons all day. We laughed, all right. At that moment a few words, simple words, came to me that are perfect for the king's song.

Dandelion

The next week of training was harder. Fleydur taught Dandelion how to hold her sword so she would not clip her feathers as she flew and how to time her wing beats between strikes in combat. When he demonstrated, his blade whistled through slivers of space between his wings.

"This is absolutely essential," said Fleydur solemnly. "Fancy flourishes mean nothing if you cannot make your sword a part of you." Fleydur gave her a dull wooden sword to practice with at first.

Dandelion gulped. "Do accidents happen often to beginners?"

"If they are too afraid," he said. "If you lose yourself to doubt and fear, for only a second, something could happen. Remember, you are in control."

After days of watching her attempt to strike with the wooden sword, Fleydur finally picked up Dandelion's steel blade. "Try now," he said, but Dandelion saw his guarded expression. He worried for her safety. Even so, Dandelion knew that this was a gesture of love. If Dandelion was to wield the weapon safely, he must dare to let her face the danger.

At the end of the lesson, Dandelion flew over.

"Fleydur," she said.

"Yes?"

"Swordplay is as much about training the mind as it is the body, isn't it?"

Fleydur's face became radiant. "Exactly!" he cried. "It is the most important thing of all."

That evening, Cloud-wing sent his reply.

Dandelion,

How is your sword training? I wish I could be there myself to watch and cheer you on. They may not admit it to anybird, but lots of the boys here were howling and crying when they first started to hold swords!

We had frost on our windows this morning, and it looked just like dandelion seeds blown from far away. Thinking of home, I started to sing the song Fleydur taught us, but the older boys shook me by the shoulder and asked if I was delirious!

Cloud-wing

Dandelion chuckled.

Cloud-wing,

Next time you duel a bird, you can burst into song—your enemies will be so shocked, they might drop their weapons. Wouldn't that be a new strategy? Fleydur's Singing Troops!

Swordplay is as much of an art as music, after all. Today I howled a bit, too, but I hope someday I can reach Rockbottom level. I wonder if I could disguise myself as a boy and go to tryouts? Would I be admitted?

In Fleydur's class, everybird's practicing our special tune. The king's birthday is almost here. I can't wait to perform, but I wish you could be with us at the Castle of Sky, too. On that evening, open your window and listen carefully. We'll be singing as loud as we can.

Dandelion

When Dandelion entered the classroom that evening, everybird was seated, but there was no sign of Trangharhad. Instead, in the front of the classroom, over the fire, hung a covered cauldron.

"Is he cooking something for us?" asked Pouldington.

The cauldron bubbled ominously.

At that moment, Tranglarhad strode in, a paper-wrapped package in his claws. He placed it on his podium, then rummaged in his suitcase and pulled out a large fork. When he looked up, nearly all the class was leaning in, trying to guess what was in his package.

The owl tapped the podium with his fork. "On your perches, now. Class begins!" Instead of talking about the package or the cauldron, he pointed the fork at the *Book of Heresy* and said, "Take out some paper and get ready to write down what I read. We will begin with a philosophy lesson. Page 295, 'On the Structure of Society.' 'The pragmatic gentlebird might speak of equality. But actually to him, bias is beautiful, prejudice popular, discrimination divine . . .'"

Tranglarhad droned on for five minutes, but every eaglet in the classroom listened to the fire and the cauldron and wondered about the package. They were so curious they could barely stay where they sat. Dandelion made a sloppy attempt to write down what Tranglarhad said, but she couldn't focus and did not know what she wrote. Finally, when Tranglarhad finished reading, Pouldington raised his wing and blurted, "What about that cauldron over there? And what is in that package, sir?"

"I was just coming to it, Pouldington," said the owl. "Now I hope you paid attention to the passage I just read. Because you will have to recite it another day." Tranglarhad picked up his package and walked to the cauldron. He licked his beak, drinking in the fear of his students.

"I am all about fairness, opportunity, and wealth," he said pleasantly. "I have in my possession several pennies. You are entitled to one if you fail to recite your passage; however, you must fetch it with your own talons."

There was a moment of confusion.

"You're paying us to *not* learn our lessons?" Pudding was incredulous.

"Correct," said Tranglarhad. He grabbed the lid of the cauldron and lifted it with a flourish, dropping a coin in. Crackling pops of heated oil sounded like explosions in the room. "It is my sizzling lose-and-gain philosophy."

"Lose?" whimpered an eaglet. "Gain?"

Tranglarhad unwrapped his package, showing to the class two plump sausages. With great care, he skewered them onto the prongs of his fork and then, quite suddenly, plunged them into the pot of hot oil and held them there.

A beak-watering smell permeated the room. It was in stark contrast to Tranglarhad's next words: "You may lose some sense of touch, some skin definitely, from this ordeal. But, oh, you gain an unforgettable experience, and if you are lucky and your toes are not fried to crisp brown sausages, you are the owner of one cent." Seeing the sausages done, Tranglarhad lifted them out of the oil. "I am sure everybird will recite quite well after a few lessons. Simple, yes?"

"What if we recite the passage perfectly?" Pudding croaked. "We get nothing?"

Unruffled, Tranglarhad held up his cooked sausages and sank his beak into them. A burst of grease spattered the lapel of his coat. Silence consumed the class as they watched the owl chomp away at his sausages, his eyes and the grease spot both glistening dangerously. "You get the pleasure of watching the fate of those who did not—is that not enough?"

Meanwhile, other ornate packages of all sorts began pouring into the castle, carried by swift falcon messengers, because the birthday of the king was fast approaching. Sigrid relished counting them, and the more she counted, brushing her claws over the ribbons and colorful wrapping paper, the wider she simpered. Her pleasure was interrupted by the sight of a plain brown package secured with yarn, somewhat dirty and wet with melted snow.

"Who has the impudence to send such rubbish?" muttered Sigrid. She picked up the package, her eyes immediately drawn to the writing scrawled on one side: TO FLEYDUR, PRINCE OF SKYTHUNDER TRIBE, SWORD MOUNTAIN. It was from a woodpecker with a name that Sigrid found peculiar and unpleasant: Ewingerale.

Why is this bird sending a package to Fleydur at the time of Morgan's birthday? she wondered.

Sigrid untied the yarn and opened the wrapping, careful not to rip the paper. She discovered a newly printed book whose green cover displayed the words *Old Scripture*. She opened it, held up the gold-rimmed glasses that had been Tranglarhad's gift to her, and read cautiously. "Waste no time and effort blindly guarding what has always been, but devote yourself instead to new ways for improvement. For a lake to be sparkling, water must flow constantly, not be stagnant."

"I am not convinced!" Sigrid said. She thought back to the time when archaeopteryxes were at the height of power. She knew it was the discipline of the Sword Mountain's rigid traditions that had helped eagles stay organized and avoid being enslaved, scattered, or forced to pay tribute. *What worked well for us then, should work well for us now*, Sigrid thought.

More and more these days, however, it seemed to her that Fleydur's popularity had robbed some eagles of their common sense. Fleydur needed to be shown that he was not infallible. Sigrid flung the book onto her table and instead read the letter in the package.

It inquired if Fleydur's plans were working well and if Fleydur would accept an invitation to celebrate the first Bright Moon Festival on the Island of Paradise. Sigrid was disappointed it did not reveal anything extreme.

Sighing, Sigrid contemplated this package. She would not give it to Fleydur right away. It might still be useful to her. She locked it in her cabinet just as a knock sounded at her door.

"Who is it?" said Sigrid with a start.

"I, Tranglarhad, Your Majesty. I am here to give my nightly reading."

"Enter," said Sigrid. She licked her beak to think of the soothing passages in the *Book of Heresy* as Tranglarhad opened the door and came into the room.

"I also wish to express my good wishes to the king, for His Majesty's birthday, as I, not being part of the court, have little opportunity to see His Majesty," he said with a bow.

Sigrid beamed. "That is very considerate of you, tutor."

"Hearing that His Majesty's health is still uncertain, I thought to present something to him—a unique medicine," said Tranglarhad. He handed Sigrid a beautifully wrapped present. She opened it and saw a small golden pill in a vial. "It's no panacea," he said, "but the wisdom of the owls may change the fate of the good king."

*Knowledge acquired under threat of force can
sleep in the inn of your mind, but will check out
in the morning.*
—FROM THE OLD SCRIPTURE

17
TENSION

On the day before the king's birthday, Fleydur went to see Morgan. Sigrid intercepted him. "Your father is busy. What do you want?"

"I want to borrow the Leasorn gemstone," said Fleydur.

"For what? The gemstone is a talisman for us eagles," she declared. "It has to be kept safe."

"I only want to show it to my students during their

last music lesson tomorrow."

Normally, Sigrid would have been appalled. But she paused and remembered some advice from the *Book of Heresy*: "*Shoot your opponents with the proverbial arrows feathered by their own plumes.*"

A smile froze on her face. "Why, yes," she said. "Yes, you may indeed. Tell the treasurer of your request tomorrow morning. Make sure the gemstone is returned without a scratch."

As Fleydur walked away, Sigrid's claws twisted the chain that held her cabinet's keys around her neck.

"Smiles, anybird?" Tranglarhad shut the door behind him. "How many of you have memorized your passage? Or are you a bunch of eager little adventurers yearning for a penny or two?"

Tranglarhad laid the *Book of Heresy* on his podium and pointed to Olga. "Please stand up."

Olga glanced frantically left and right.

"Yes, you, Miss Olga," said the owl. "You may start our delightful evening—I've heard that you have a lovely, loud voice."

Olga stood up unsteadily, touching her frilly cap.

"Page 295, 'On the Structure of Society,'" prompted Tranglarhad.

Olga swallowed. "'On the Structure of Society.' 'The pragmatic gentlebird might speak of equality,'" she said waveringly, "'but actually to him, bias is beautiful, prejudice popular, discrimination . . . divine . . .'"

"Ah, yes, praise be!" murmured the owl. "Do continue."

"'The world must have a stratified order, as clear as . . . as clear as day and night. The detested spawn of those with low rank shall . . .'" Olga's voice was shaking. Her eyes, downcast, were wet. She gripped the sides of her desk. "'. . . shall remain servants. M-m-merit . . .'" She broke off, silently crying, as the cauldron crackled with oil.

"'Is nothing,'" snarled Tranglarhad. "Repeat this line again, clearly: 'Merit is nothing. Birth is everything.'"

Olga hid her face in her wing and shook her head.

Tranglarhad's face darkened. He opened the cauldron's lid and beckoned to Olga.

"Don't move, Olga," Dandelion said.

"Oh?" said Tranglarhad. "Will you take her place, then?" He leered. "Will you stand up for a mountain topper? A summit bird?"

Dandelion's claws closed around the candle in her pocket. She stood up. Her heart hammered. "I will. We are all eaglets of Sword Mountain." She swallowed. "Sir, do you believe what the *Book of Heresy* says?"

Tranglarhad smirked. "Isn't it what life on Sword Mountain's summit shows?"

"Do you believe that merit is nothing?" asked Dandelion. "Didn't your merit as a teacher earn you this post?"

Tranglarhad stared back at Dandelion.

"Then do you believe in merit for yourself but deny it for everybird else?" she went on.

Doesn't everybird? thought Tranglarhad. For a moment, it was a relief to inflict on others the wounds he himself had suffered. But it was no time to let an argument with this princess take over the class. It might spoil his favor with the queen.

Tranglarhad threw a piece of chalk into the cauldron.

"Dismissed!" he shouted, and was the first to walk out.

Cloud-wing, if you could see this now, Dandelion thought.

She was still standing. And she realized that the eaglets stood with her.

Making the most of every celebration? A piece of cake.
—FROM THE *BOOK OF HERESY*

18
THE KING'S BIRTHDAY

Winter clamped rows of glittering teeth over the castle's windows. By day the icicles dripped slowly and sparkled under the cold white sun. By night they lengthened and sharpened.

As the flags of the castle strained to be free, snow-flakes fell and softened the edges of the mountain. Sword Cliff was covered in a sheath of immaculate snow.

The king awoke and thought, *My birthday! Today's the only day of the year when a ruler can have fun.*

Then he thought, *I am too old for fun.* It was unhappy to be reminded of old age in such a dreary, cold season.

"Morgan? Do you realize, it's been a hundred—"

"A hundred seasons that the mountain wind has carried me, yes," he said with a sigh. "Oh, Sigrid, all is well! I am fine, the kingdom is recovering. Why the long face?" The king looked merry. "Somebird's planning to send me a coffin as a birthday present, is that it?"

Sigrid brought the king's daily cocktail of medicines, along with the golden pill. "Take some medicine for your health, at least," she said.

Dandelion got up at dawn and opened her door to see the castle transformed.

All the corridors were decked with purple banners that read HURRAH FOR THE KING! in gold letters. The faint buzz of voices coming from elsewhere in the castle thrilled Dandelion: The visitors had come. After donning formal dress, she flew down the spiral staircase, meeting Fleydur along the way. "It'll be your first official appearance as the princess," he said. "Come down to the hall."

Olga came by and approached Dandelion.

"Dandelion, for what you did in class yesterday . . ." She looked at the ribbons tied on her feet. "I just wanted to say thanks."

"You're welcome," said Dandelion.

"And . . ." Olga's voice trailed off. As they turned a corner, she blurted, "I'm sorry. For the things I did when you were sick. All of that, fake party and—"

Dandelion extended a wing. "And now we're going to a real party."

Olga touched her wing tip to Dandelion's, and they flew side by side.

"Are you nervous?" she asked Dandelion. "You know we're going to perform this evening."

"I'm only excited," Dandelion said.

Eagles were packed into the banquet hall. The barons of other peaks in the mountain range were all there, and their children, who wore silver acorns on their collars instead of gold. Ambassadors from other tribes, and artisans, merchants, and farmers of Sword Mountain, mingled among them. Dandelion had never seen such a crowd before.

Though the king had not yet made his appearance, the hall was full of activity. More birthday presents arrived by the minute, despite the mountains of gifts there already. Cooks bustled in and out with plates balanced on their heads. The castle staff rolled in barrels of cider and pulled a cart full of bottles of champagne. Watching everything, joy and excitement buoyed Dandelion so much that she felt she was rising to the chandeliers.

It was truly a perfect day for Fleydur's concert. Everybird was in a generous, merry mood. Even the advisers let the *Handbook of the Feathered Aristocrat* slip from their minds, for there was not one bird who was not grinning or laughing, and a lot of beaks were open wider than thirty degrees.

A herald ran into the hall, cupped his talons near his bill, and shouted, "His Majesty is coming!"

All the birds flew into the air. "The king! The king! Our beloved king!" they chanted.

In a ceremonial gown of purple and white, a sword strapped to one side, a silver pen to the other, and a scepter in his claws, Morgan cried to the gathered crowd of well-wishers, "Thank you! It's a day to remember!"

He stood in the banquet hall, feeling the cheers fill his frail body with new life. He would need a lot of energy to get through the activities of the day. He'd had a headache earlier, after his talk with Sigrid, but he was feeling better at last.

"Thank you all, birds of Skythunder, friends of Skythunder. I am honored that so many have come to celebrate my old age with me. I need not say more, for I know many of you are waiting for the cake!"

Morgan gestured toward the center of the hall, where there was a chocolate cake.

In truth, it was a mountain of goodness—a replica of Sword Mountain itself, crafted by a ten-eagle team of royal bakers and confectioners supervised by a sculptor. The day before, the undercooks had whitewashed the slopes of the cake with tubs of vanilla icing. They'd dusted green sprinkles on the base to mimic evergreen trees and capped the peak with shredded coconut that they'd bought from seagull traders. Ninety-nine candles of gold, purple, and green crowned its ledges. The hundredth candle, on the top of the cake, was shaped like Sword Cliff. So beautiful and beak watering it was that, for fear of thieves and pantry raiders, a platoon of guards had paced around the cake all night.

Now it towered above everything else in the banquet hall, ample and majestic upon a platter as big as a fountain, and every pair of eyes in the Castle of Sky flickered to it longingly. Not only because the cake itself would be heavenly—

"There is a wish coin baked into the cake," Olga said in a hoarse whisper to Dandelion. "If your slice of cake has the coin, the king himself will grant you one wish!

Anything, anything within his law and his power."

Dandelion was open beaked.

"What would you wish for?" asked Olga.

"Me?" said Dandelion. "I . . . I'd wish for . . ." She was already so content it was hard to think of anything more. She had friends, like Cloud-wing and Olga here, and family, like Fleydur. She had a home. She could wish for Fleydur's music school to become permanent. However, she remembered that the Iron Nest also had a say in the matter, and Morgan couldn't grant that by himself. If she got the wish coin, she could ask for a chance to go to the Rockbottom Academy.

"Shut the curtains! It's time for the lighting!" Everybird quieted as various birds of rank were given the honor of lighting the many candles on the mountain.

Dandelion's eyes slowly drifted down the miniature mountain as, one by one, the candles glowed, and she found the familiar outlines of the cliff where her family's cave was. There was a candle there, too! She touched her own candle in her pocket, and it seemed to feel warm as well.

Morgan flew around the cake, spiraling to the very top. All the birds sucked in their breath with the king. He blew at the Sword Cliff candle. The flame merely flickered. Morgan frowned. He sucked in a deeper breath and puffed. In the middle he suddenly broke off, coughing painfully.

"Are you all right, Your Majesty?" asked the physician.

"Just the chill, just the chill," insisted the king, finally puffing once more and blowing out the candle. He looked dubiously at the ninety-nine candles left. Then he raised his head and said with smile, "Come, let us do this together."

Dandelion felt a glow in her heart. In this moment, the hundreds of eagles gathered here were like one huge family. They pressed up close to the cake, and all their breaths combined into one gust that put out the flames. The curtains were opened again. Tendrils of blue smoke curled toward the ceiling.

"Announcements, Your Majesty?" said Amicus, the secretary of the court.

"I declare," said King Morgan, "I am starving!"

The eagles could already imagine the first bite of cake melting deliciously on the tongue.

Sigrid twitched nervously as she observed the distribution. The top layer went to the king. The rest of the cake was divided up and served according to rank, or birds received the slice of the mountain corresponding to where they actually lived.

Sigrid wanted the wish coin so much that her talons made indentations in the plate she clutched. She knew what she'd wish for; she'd already written it down on a slip of paper—"Let Forlath be the heir to the throne of Sword Mountain, and let Fleydur go elsewhere to spread his ideas."

Sigrid grabbed a trident-sized fork and ate her slice voraciously, crumbs clinging to her feathers. But her piece was a generous portion. She picked up a carving knife and hacked the rest of her slice into crumbs, trying to find something solid. Nothing!

Oh, who has the coin? thought Sigrid, desperate. *Is it that valley bird, Dandelion?*

The only comfort was that Fleydur did not seem to have the coin either. The tradition was that the lucky bird would step forth sometime during the party to present a wish to the king. Many birds ate leisurely as they conversed, a nibble every few sentences.

The wait was driving Sigrid crazy.

*Music makes a thousand hearts beat in
rhythm together.*
—FROM THE OLD SCRIPTURE

19
THE COMMON THREAD

Can you believe it's over?"

"The last music lesson."

"And then the performance."

"And then . . ."

"Nothing. Nothing till tomorrow, when the Iron Nest votes."

Dandelion listened to the eaglets around her whisper. They were all gathered early in the small rehearsal room for a brief meeting, a short final lesson, before mounting the stage and singing to the king.

"Do any of you have the wish coin?" asked Dandelion.

"We can wish something for the music school," added Olga. Everybird shook their heads.

"The king can't make that kind of decision without the Iron Nest," said Pudding.

"Oh, surely, surely we could wish something—to continue our music lessons, at least!" said Olga.

But since none of them had the coin, it didn't matter what they might have asked for.

When Fleydur entered, the room fell into silence. He was clutching a small box, and two armed guards of the king stuck their heads into the room before nodding and closing the door.

Pudding recognized the guards as those of the treasury. He pointed at the box. "Fleydur, is that . . ."

Fleydur opened the box and took out the Leasorn gem, whose light bathed the faces of the students in wavering ripples of indigo, violet, and lavender.

"The stone that belongs to no treasury, but to everybird," he whispered.

He said to the Leasorn, "Sing my heart." The gem responded with the cheery tune that Fleydur first taught them. Smiling, Fleydur extended the gem toward the eaglets.

Dandelion understood. "Sing my heart," she said.

Olga followed suit. "Sing my heart."

"And mine," said Pudding, and all the eaglets chimed in. The tune of each eaglet built upon the rest, adding new harmonies.

As the final eaglet breathlessly whispered the magical words, they found themselves listening to a full-fledged symphony. The eaglets looked at one another, astonished.

Above the music, Fleydur spoke. "Tonight, children, represents how far we've come. This was unthinkable mere seasons ago. Just look at each of you; weren't you strangers to each other then? Restrained by rigid traditions, bound by the angle of your beaks. But now, with new eyes, new ears, you've discovered friends in those around you. You've found the eaglet in yourselves. Yes, music is the common thread that links us all. Together, you've grown; together, you've flourished. This is why I want to give music lessons and build a music school," he said, and then, smiling, beckoned to them. "Come, my children, they're waiting for us!"

Stepping onto the stage, wing in wing, Fleydur and his students began the first happy birthday song to the king in the history of Sword Mountain. *The Castle of Sky was built for a chorus to sing here,* Dandelion thought. The large domed hall had been waiting for music to fill its space, and now the air shimmered with the opening notes.

The eagles of the audience leaned toward the music. Morgan listened, tears glistening in his eyes. Even the members of the Iron Nest took off their caps, although they and the more traditional eagles sat there somewhat awkwardly.

The birds of Sword Mountain could not stay silent for long. Eagles began to join in, and it didn't matter that they'd never sung before; it didn't matter that their voices were a little off-key.

When the song ended, the birds sat still, in a daze. The smattering of applause soon became full-fledged. "Thank you. That was just . . ." King Morgan shook his head as he placed a set of talons over his chest, unable to find the words to express his feelings. Fleydur led his students in a slow bow.

And then they sang the song that they, under Dandelion's direction, had written themselves.

Open your beaks
Sing a song

Open your hearts
From now on.

From the mountain peak
Let our voices grow;
Hear the answer
From valleys below.

In one another,
Echoes of ourselves
Sisters and brothers
Beyond acorn shells . . .

Dandelion watched as hundreds of eagles swayed to the singing. They were like a sea, rippling with waves of serene faces. Their music was responsible for this, she realized, awed and humbled. Her words, their own tune. She and the other eaglets singing along with her—*they* had created this happiness!

Though it was winter outside, she sensed, as she sang, a spring thaw in the hearts of the audience. *If only you were here, Cloud-wing!* she thought.

Afterward, as everybird refreshed themselves with drinks and more cake, Morgan brought up the question.

"The winner? Who has the wish coin?"

Sigrid strained her neck, peering in all directions. The crowd murmured and moved, and there was some confusion, and then a short-legged, triangular-headed figure stood up.

"I do, Your Majesty."

Tranglarhad the owl beamed.

Sigrid had forgotten about him. Her hunger for the coin overpowered her partiality for the tutor. She could only watch in wrath as the owl shuffled toward the king, displaying a glinting silver coin left and right to muttering doubters. His expression was one of utmost humility.

Inside, however, Tranglarhad's emotions were churning.

This is my time to act! he thought. How could he best use the wish coin to get hold of the Leasorn gem?

He could ask for the gem itself, but the king probably didn't have the legal power to give away a national treasure. He could just ask to *see* the gemstone, but there were hundreds of birds here, all witnesses. If the gem later disappeared, they would know who had taken it. Though he could formally ask for the eagles to stay away from the old mine beneath the mountain, that might draw more attention to the mine. *Oh, holy hoot,* he thought.

Perhaps it was safer to wish for something else,

but . . . could he pass up this chance? Tranglarhad took a deep breath.

Still a decision could not be made. After he had found out he had the coin, Tranglarhad had written a wish about the Leasorn, and a second wish, on two pieces of paper, and he had put the first in his right pocket, the other in his left.

As he walked closer, he debated again with each heavy step.

Right or left? Right or left?

In front of the king, Tranglarhad stuck his talons in his pockets. He closed his eyes as he searched slowly. A few long, anguished seconds later, he fished out a grubby rolled-up piece of paper from his left pocket. Mumbling civilities and bowing, he placed it and the coin in the claws of the king.

Everybird watched as Morgan unrolled the paper with some difficulty.

The king's eyes glided across the paper. He stiffened. His eyes rolled slowly upward and his head drooped to one side, a raspy moan coming from his open beak.

"Your Majesty!" shouted the physician.

"Father!" called Fleydur.

"No!" Forlath cried out.

The crowd bellowed, "What did you wish for?"

As birds pushed in from all sides, Tranglarhad shielded himself with his claws. "No, I didn't—I didn't have . . . I only . . . I . . ." The owl huddled against a wall. "I j-just wished t-the king—"

Morgan stirred, shaking his head as if waking from a nightmare. "Stop, I'm all right!" he said. "It's nothing, a faint headache or some such, I've had it on and off today since breakfast, but I'm quite fine. My apologies," he said to the owl, who nodded numbly.

"Why, this is the first time ever in my reign that a bird did not ask me for something for himself!" The king looked kindly at the owl. "You are the new tutor, aren't you?"

Tranglarhad nodded again.

"It is fortunate that we have birds like you," boomed the king. "Thank you." Turning toward the expectant and still angry crowd, he read from the paper. "May the king have good health and long life."

Applause filled the banquet hall.

"Aye, to the king!" Tranglarhad laughed nervously and raised a glass. His eyes met Morgan's. "To the king!"

Morgan felt weary in his bones. The headache crept upon him again, worse this time. Perhaps it was the effects of champagne, or the noise, or maybe he was just too old and tired. "Sigrid," he said slowly.

"What is it, Morgan?"

"I want to return to my room."

"But the celebration's far from over."

"Yes, but I just decided something," said Morgan. "I think—I think I need to start on my will."

Sigrid stood up immediately, helping Morgan stand. He was swaying now. "You stay here, my dear," he told Sigrid. "Don't worry about me."

"His Majesty King Morgan is retiring to his chambers!" announced a herald.

"Oh, go on and continue to enjoy yourselves. It's a royal order," Morgan said. He was assisted out of the banquet hall.

"Well, then, we should ring the life gong early, shouldn't we?" asked a member of the castle staff.

According to tradition, on the night of a king's birthday, a special gong would be struck once for every season of the king's age, with an interval of ten seconds between strikes. For Morgan this year, there were would be a hundred beats.

"You may start," said Sigrid.

But she wasn't thinking of gongs or age. She was thinking about the will Morgan had just said he would write. The king had actually seemed to enjoy Fleydur's foolish concert. Suppose, just suppose he chose Fleydur as his heir. And now that Fleydur's concert had been so well received, the Iron Nest might even side with him. Then it wouldn't be long before Fleydur would, vote by vote, reshape the mountain!

Sigrid could not allow this monstrosity to happen. She didn't have the wish coin today, but she did have a backup plan ready. It was riskier, but, by the *Book of Heresy*, she would see it through.

As she walked past a guard on her way back to her seat, her face staring straight ahead, she whispered, "Fleydur's package."

The guard nodded curtly, signaled to a companion, and the two glided off.

Sigrid smiled at her son Forlath. "It's a wonderful night, isn't it?"

As they settled in their seats to watch the rest of the concert, they all heard the first gong strike.

When a talon strikes a mirror, a spiderweb of cracks blooms.
—FROM THE BOOK OF HERESY

20
WITHIN A HUNDRED BEATS

Meanwhile, Tranglarhad had retreated to a corner.

Was that a chance lost? Was it? he wondered between beats of the gong. Each time the thought came to him, he raised his glass and gulped a beakful of cold water to calm down.

His wish, though, had not gone completely to waste. Touched by Tranglarhad's unselfishness, the treasurer sought to join the tutor by his corner near the door. Tranglarhad noticed the treasurer had had a little too much champagne. After draining another bubbly glass, the treasurer blurted, "Remember our talk? About my son?"

Tranglarhad nearly choked on his water. "How could I forget it?"

"It was removed," said the treasurer thickly. "For Fleydur's music students to see, in the rehearsal room. Just before the performance. Didn't you want to take a look at it?"

This was all Tranglarhad needed to know.

"More champagne, good tutor?" the treasurer said.

"Oh, no," said the owl. "I must, er, plan; yes, plan. For my class. It starts within the hour." Tranglarhad hurriedly refilled the treasurer's glass before he rose and left.

"How dutiful! You are a paragon of virtue," said the treasurer, tears glistening on his face. "I am glad that my son is under your guidance."

Tranglarhad slipped away from the banquet hall, flinging a cloak he had hidden under his tutor robes around himself and pulling up the hood. On ghost wings he quickly caught up to Sigrid's guards. One of them was carrying a package.

They paused in front of the rehearsal room where Fleydur had held his final music lesson. Tranglarhad hung back, hiding behind one of the birthday banners on the wall. More birds were in the room!

The treasury guards inside smiled to be relieved so soon, and hurried toward the celebration, flying right under Tranglarhad.

From an intersection, the sound of more wing beats carried to the owl. This time, Fleydur and Dandelion came around a corner and headed in the direction of the rehearsal room.

The treasury guards saluted as they passed. "Evening, Prince Fleydur!"

Fleydur returned their greeting. Tranglarhad grew tense, afraid that Dandelion might glance up and notice the owl-shaped bulge behind the birthday banner, but she and Fleydur took another turn and flew away.

Relieved, the owl redirected his ears toward voices now coming from the open rehearsal room.

"Here it is."

"What did the queen say? Put it into the package?"

Tranglarhad sucked in his breath, resisting the urge to dash forward and peek. "Patience," he said to himself.

He pressed back into an alcove in the wall as Sigrid's soldiers emerged in the hallway. The package they carried looked more stuffed. "You hear something?" said one eagle.

"Just the gong," said the other. "We have to be quick." They headed toward the other side of the castle, and Tranglarhad followed them, the three birds moving in a triangle. They went through the Hall of Mirrors.

Had the two soldiers even glanced at a mirror, they could have seen the owl, tagging along behind them. Tranglarhad felt dizzy as he noted hundreds of Tranglarhads in the reflections, sneaking alongside him.

The guards finally stopped before a half-open door near the top of the south tower. They entered, placed the package on the desk, and left.

Tranglarhad waited in the shadows, his eyes gleaming. The vibrations of the gong beats tingled in his blood. The owl rushed into the study, flipped the package upside down, and slit it open. The Leasorn gem! He tossed the book that had also been inside the package onto Fleydur's desk; the silk cloth that had been wrapped around the gem fluttered to the floor. He thrust the shining, faceted prize into his pocket and made for the door.

The gong beats had masked approaching claw steps. Uri, Fleydur's valet, was not far away down the hall. "Hey! Who are you?" Uri hollered.

Tranglarhad jumped into the air, pulling out a cleaver. He would not lose this one precious chance! He slashed at Uri as he rushed past. Uri drew his own weapon and struck off the tip of one of Tranglarhad's talons. Biting back his hoot of pain, the owl fled into the depths of the castle. Astounded, the valet did not chase him.

Back in his office, Tranglarhad hurriedly changed into a loose-fitting suit, dropping the gem into a hidden pocket over his heart. As he tried to swab his toe, a knock sounded at his door. Tranglarhad jumped.

"Tutor?" said the treasurer. "I realize you are going to your lesson. I want to talk more about my son's studies as we go down the hall. You don't mind?"

"Not at all, not at all," said the owl. He managed to put on a wavering smile. He must stay for the lesson and avoid suspicion.

Morgan had sent a messenger for Fleydur and Dandelion. As the celebration continued, the two made their way toward the king's tower.

"That was wonderful, the performance you put on with your students, Fleydur," exclaimed Morgan. "I am proud of you and your music. I am proud of how you adopted this eaglet and showed us something extraordinary." He gazed at Dandelion. "The children of the court, they were gloomy miniature adults, never children, until today. And the adults? They were unchanging iron statues, never alive, until today."

He placed a set of talons gently over Fleydur's. In the distance, the gong continued to sound.

"You are a born leader, Fleydur. Won't you stay?"

"I—I will stay until I know I have done enough to help Sword Mountain."

"Does my 'enough' differ much from yours? For I think there's something a king—"

Uri rushed into the king's room.

"Your Majesty, I've urgent news for Prince Fleydur!" cried Uri. When Morgan acknowledged him, he turned to his master. "Prince, there was an intruder in your room a minute ago! I tried to stop him, but he fled!"

"Who was he, could you tell?"

The valet shook his head. "He was hidden in a cloak and armed. But I cut off a talon nail." He showed it to Fleydur. Dandelion and Fleydur both stared at it. The nail could have been anybird's.

"What did he take?" asked Fleydur.

"I don't know," Uri said. "But I do know that some birds dropped off a package for you earlier. Come quick, sir!" The gong rang as if to punctuate his remark.

"Strange," Fleydur muttered as Morgan nodded and

allowed him to leave. "Dandelion, you go to class now."
He followed his valet into his study. Nothing was astray,
nothing missing. Then he noticed the open package on
his desk. "What's this?"

Fleydur pulled the book from the wrapping. "How
fantastic! A printed copy of the *Old Scripture*, from my
old woodpecker friend Winger . . ." Engrossed, he dismissed the incident of the intruder.

Dandelion was nearly late to class, but this time, the owl
tutor did not seem to mind a student's tardiness.

"Good hiding—er, good evening class," he said.

Pudding raised a claw.

"Yes, Pouldington?"

"Mr. Tranglarhad, sir, you've buttoned your suit
wrong," said Pudding. Tranglarhad glanced down,
alarmed to find it was true.

"Yes, yes," he said, flustered and annoyed. He turned
to one side, undoing the buttons and fixing the problem.
As his talons danced rapidly over his suit, Dandelion saw
something that made her suck in her breath.

Tranglarhad looked sharply at her. "Oh . . . ah . . .
ah-choo!" said Dandelion.

The owl relaxed, blinking rapidly, and turned to the
class to begin his lesson.

Dandelion didn't listen to a word. The gong rang. Her heart pounded.

One of the owl's talon nails was missing.

"The gemstone is gone! The gemstone is gone!" somebird cried in the banquet hall. The birds of the court leaped up as a rush of guards stampeded toward the treasury. "Block the doors! Close the gates!"

"How is it possible?"

"Who stole from the treasury?"

"When was the gemstone last seen?"

The treasurer, coming back from Tranglarhad's classroom, sobered up immediately from the hysteria. To his dismay, he could not remember the details of the evening, apart from meeting the tutor in his office. The treasurer stammered, bewildered. "Prince Fleydur borrowed the gem to show it to his students earlier this evening."

"Where is it now?"

"We don't know!"

"It's not in their rehearsal room."

The hall was boiling with voices.

"It wasn't returned!" shouted the queen at the same moment the gong struck again. She stood and pointed toward Fleydur's tower. "He is responsible!

Ask him!" Birds holding torches flew up the spiral staircase.

Tranglarhad dropped the chalk from his claws as he heard the alarm. *Calm, now, calm,* he thought to himself. The students jumped off their perches, their lesson promptly forgotten. Tranglarhad opened the door just as a stream of soldiers swooped past. Tranglarhad stopped one. "Pray tell, what is this uproar?" he said.

"Don't let your students out yet, sir! Somebird has stolen the gemstone of the mountain!"

"Who did it?" cried Tranglarhad, blinking with horror.

"Don't know. It may be one of the princes," said the soldier as he left. Tranglarhad closed the classroom door, his face solemn and glum as he latched it shut. As the confusion of shouts and fluttering wings and crackling torches went past, Tranglarhad bellowed to his class, "A shocking thing has happened on the mountain!"

He stomped up and down the rows of the desks, piercing each pupil with his gaze. "Stealing is a treacherous, hideous, abominable act. Do you hear me? How many of you have stolen something, even a crumb of food?" Beneath his feathers, Tranglarhad's face was dark red. "Be ashamed of yourself! It is wrong to take something that is not yours." As he spun around, he could feel the weight of the gemstone against the secret pocket over his heart.

"Tonight—this scandal—let this be a lesson!" A beat of the gong rang after his final word.

It was easy to declare an emergency and end class early. None of the worried parents who swarmed into the classroom noticed or cared when Tranglarhad slipped away from the castle. Cauldron hanging from one claw, the *Book of Heresy* in the other, the owl turned his head around for a last furtive look at the summit. The layer of snow that covered Sword Cliff like a sheath had crumpled off. Underneath, the gray granite, sharp and shining and gilded with ice, blazed in the moonlight like a bared blade. Tranglarhad smiled a smile nobird saw. He and his gliding shadow on the white snow seemed to gradually merge into one as he descended toward the foot of the mountain.

Sigrid kept close behind the flood of fear-stricken eagles. "Hoy!" shouted the guards, banging at the door to Fleydur's study.

"What do you want?" cried Uri.

"Open up!" the crowd yelled back.

The door creaked open, and Fleydur stood there, his

face gaunt in the torchlight. "What?"

"Search his room. Is he hiding the gemstone?"

Fleydur staggered back, gripping the *Old Scripture*, as the eagles flew past him and started pulling out his drawers, yanking back the curtains, flinging books off his shelves, and rummaging in his closet. And still the gong rang on.

Sigrid hung back in the shadows, clutching her shawl around her, her heart beating wildly.

"I've found something!" called out one of the soldiers. All activity stopped. The soldier lifted a silk cloth from the floor behind Fleydur's desk.

"It's the cloth that was wrapped around the gemstone!"

Sigrid stepped up. "But where is the stone itself?"

Fleydur shook his head slowly, not comprehending. "I don't have it."

The strike of the gong was loud in the silence that followed.

"You do. You should!" Sigrid accused him. "The cloth is here. The gem has to be in your room!"

"He's hiding it," insisted somebird.

"I took nothing; I left the gemstone in the rehearsal room, with the guards! Haven't they taken it back?" cried Fleydur.

Sigrid squinted triumphantly. "With your own trick,

we'll know if the gem is nearby. Tell the Leasorn to sing your heart!"

Fleydur reluctantly did, but there was no response.

"Fleydur didn't do it," added Uri. "It must have been that thief who planted that cloth here. I cut his talon, see?" The valet showed everybird the fragment of nail.

Sigrid's heart did a somersault. The gemstone was now truly gone. Things were beginning to slip out of her talons. But perhaps it was all for the better, she reasoned to herself. Now Fleydur would be truly condemned.

"Your Majesty, what will we do? Shall we inform the king?" said one of the eagles.

"No. Not yet," said the queen.

Then a messenger burst into the room. "The king!" he shouted, his eyes wide with horror. "The king is dead!"

And then nothing. Nobird spoke a word. Even the air they breathed felt as if something was dreadfully amiss. And they realized that the one hundred beats were done, and the gong, like a heart, had gone silent.

In the airless vacuum left by fear, reason suffocates.
—FROM THE OLD SCRIPTURE

21
OUT OF CONTROL

The banquet hall, as Dandelion flew past, had
been abandoned. Only a few of the castle staff
hurried here and there. The sound of their
work clearing plates and forks echoed like the clattering
of bones.

She'd sensed the clamor wind its way up to Fleydur's
tower. After class had abruptly ended and eaglets had
been whisked off by agitated parents, Dandelion had

already started to hear piercing cries from the king's tower.

Eagles were streaming in the corridors. The physician brushed past Dandelion and sped toward the king's tower. "Can't be, his health was better . . . can't die . . ."

When she had turned back to confront Tranglarhad, the owl had vanished. Now the next best thing to do was to find and inform Fleydur. She listened for noises from Fleydur's tower. There was no more shouting. As she neared his study, Fleydur's valet appeared in the doorway.

"He's been arrested, Dandelion," Uri croaked.

"What?" cried Dandelion. "You don't mean for—"

"Yes, they say he's the gemstone thief!" said Uri bitterly.

Dandelion threw her claws in the air. "How can he be? He has no reason to steal the gemstone! And he couldn't have been the intruder in his own room. Tranglarhad's the thief. Just now in class, one of his nails was missing. He's left the castle."

"Nasty piece of work, that owl," the valet said darkly. "But how can we prove he did it if he's gone?"

Dandelion needed somebird who had power to listen to her. *Queen Sigrid hired Tranglarhad,* she remembered.

Maybe she'll know where he might have gone. To be sure, Sigrid did not like Dandelion much, but surely the queen would want to find the true thief and recover the eagles' Leasorn gem. "Do you think the queen will help me?" Dandelion asked the valet.

"No, don't go! The danger—"

"I have to do something!"

Dandelion swung around and flew down the hall toward the queen's chamber, hoping to find answers. Entering without knocking, she peered about in the gloom of the antechamber.

"Your Majesty?" Dandelion called out. She saw only abandoned teacups. She heard a sound behind her. The hummingbird handmaid was there.

"Where's Fleydur, do you know?" she asked. "I need to see him."

The hummingbird made a gesture of shackles and then pointed at the floor below. Dandelion's heart sank.

"Who's talking in there?"

Dandelion spun around. Sigrid was in the hall.

"Fleydur's innocent!" said Dandelion.

"Get out," said the queen.

"He didn't steal the gemstone, Your Majesty—"

"Get out!"

"—I know who did."

The queen froze. "What?" she said. Dandelion explained.

"Impossible." Sigrid's eyes widened. She swayed on her feet.

"But he's disappeared. You know Mr. Tranglarhad, Your Majesty—"

"Enough!" shouted Sigrid, her feathers puffed up in rage. "You accuse Tranglarhad, an esteemed educator, of such a heinous crime? Not one more word, you hear?"

"But I—"

"You have no right to talk back to me. Especially since you are no princess. Your title is revoked since the arrest of Fleydur." The queen snatched the gold circlet from Dandelion's head.

"Your Majesty!" begged Dandelion.

"You have no power or place here," said Sigrid. "Whatever you know amounts to nothing."

Convinced that she'd get no help from the queen, Dandelion flew out of the room, banging the door behind her.

"Leave this mountaintop once and for all!" screeched the queen behind her.

Dandelion dashed up to her chamber. Injustice was not unfamiliar to her now. The only way to deal with it was to prove Fleydur was innocent. Though her heart was with Fleydur, she knew that even if she yelled herself hoarse and cried herself blind, she could not help him at all. She needed to take action on his behalf. If there was a trial, it would be impossible for her to testify for Fleydur effectively with Sigrid in control. Dandelion needed to track down Tranglarhad and retrieve the gemstone. It was the only way she knew out of this living nightmare.

Dandelion considered asking Olga, Pudding, or some of the other eaglets to join her. *But no,* she thought. *Though they love Fleydur, they aren't trained to fight. It is too much to ask of them. I cannot lead them away from their families and into danger.* As Dandelion tied Wind-voice's sword to her side with Cloud-wing's rope, she told herself that she was not afraid of what lay beyond the mountain. She would not hesitate to leave the safety of the castle, if she could save somebird's life.

She would go to Rockbottom. Cloud-wing was trained in swordplay and had friends there who could fight as well. He could help her rescue Fleydur.

Sigrid flew toward the king's tower. Emotions boiled inside the queen's chest, but the dominant one was painful incredulity.

Morgan cannot be dead!

She burst into the king's room. The physician and the castle staff tried to dissuade her, but she pushed past. Morgan was perched by an open window, his back to her, leaning over a piece of paper on his desk. He had a quill in his talons. And blood, a thin trickle of it, dripped, dripped, dripped from his beak.

A strange, twisted cry came from Sigrid's throat.

She rushed forward to touch Morgan on his shoulder. At the slight pressure he collapsed backward into her wings, his head lolling. His eyes were glazed, half closed, an expression of faint surprise in them.

Sigrid hugged her husband's body close to her. She glanced back at the blood-spattered paper and saw with shock what had been blocked from her sight by Morgan's body. One word scrawled in hasty, slanted writing, in the agony of death: FLEYDUR.

Was Morgan showing who had killed him?

At the emergency assembly, snow lashed the windows. The dead king's spirit seemed to linger and moan in anguish from every corner. Even through the walls, they heard a high singing noise, a horrible sound that went on and off like the whetting of a blade—the wind shrieking as the sharpened edge of Sword Cliff cut into it.

Torchlight flickered. Fleydur stood on the black-and-white checkered floor. Faces of those in the Iron Nest were fixed upon him, glimmering with tears. Only fifteen advisers were present in their chessboard formation. A court replacement for Simplicio had not been found, but there was no gap—Sigrid stood, leading the Iron Nest. In a widow's black satin dress and a black veil, with a coral brooch glittering like a drop of blood at her throat, the queen pointed an accusing talon toward Fleydur.

"Let me see Father, please. . . ." Fleydur was sobbing softly.

"Are you happy now? With what you've done?" said Sigrid, gritting her beak.

"Order!" shouted the secretary, Amicus. "Your Majesty, there are two charges made against Prince Fleydur," he said, his voice shaking. He had to take a deep breath to continue. "First, the murder of the late king, a double offense: regicide and patricide. Second, the theft of the greatest treasure of the kingdom." Through his own tears, he surveyed the members of the court. "As the king is no longer with us, by law we cannot hold trial for one as high as a prince."

"Continue on. Somebird else must become king," said the treasurer.

Another adviser spoke. "Who? The king left no complete will."

"Then the eldest son—" began the general.

"No!" screamed Sigrid. "You cannot crown a crim—"

She stopped herself, took a deep breath, and addressed Fleydur without facing him. "You are under suspicion, Fleydur. You cannot ascend the throne unless you are proven to be innocent."

Fleydur looked dazed. His beak opened soundlessly.

Glancing at Fleydur, Amicus frowned with uncertainty. "Then in order for tonight's trial to continue, we will ask the next in line for the throne, Prince Forlath, to assume temporary power."

"Yes," said Sigrid.

"No, I can't! I won't be able to . . . ," said Forlath. He lowered his head under Sigrid's gaze. "If . . . if I must," he whispered.

Noting that the theft seemed to have occurred before the king's death, the secretary turned to the subject of the gemstone, to get a better sense of how the night had unfolded. Like the snow heaping outside, evidence against Fleydur mounted. Numerous birds testified to his early departure from the hall, before the end of the birthday celebration. Two birds confirmed that they had seen Fleydur heading toward the rehearsal room.

"Do you recognize these birds, Fleydur?" Sigrid asked.

Fleydur nodded. "I saw them earlier this evening."

"We were guarding the gemstone in the rehearsal room, during the performance," declared one guard. "At intermission, two other guards relieved us. Just as we were leaving the door and headed for the banquet hall, we met Fleydur going in the opposite direction."

"But I wasn't going to the rehearsal room," said Fleydur. "I was going to see Father." He was met with disbelieving looks. "Why would I want to steal the gem anyway?" he pleaded. "Why would I steal from my own tribe?"

A scholar beat his wings at Fleydur. "I overheard my grandson discussing Fleydur's last music lesson. He said that Fleydur believed that the Leasorn gem is not ours and shouldn't be in our treasury!"

"Guards from the second shift, step forward," ordered Amicus. "How was the gem stolen while you were on guard?"

The queen listened as her hired birds rehearsed the answer she concocted. "We believe we were tricked. Fleydur's valet acted as the decoy, by crying about an intruder in the castle and begging our help! When we returned, the gem was gone. We were lured."

"And don't forget, the gemstone cloth was found in Fleydur's room," Sigrid added.

"Now answer me truthfully, Fleydur," said Amicus. "Where is the gemstone now?"

"I don't know," said Fleydur.

"He won't admit to the theft." Sigrid turned to the

secretary. "Ask him about King Morgan's death!"

"The staff in the king's tower said that you came over to see the king tonight, correct?" said Amicus.

Fleydur nodded.

"They tell us that you and your adopted daughter visited the king after he left the banquet hall. The king was fine before you came. They say he died shortly after you left. What went on between the two of you?"

"He told me how he loved the music. He wanted to know if I would stay."

"Oh, really?" Sigrid said. "Then what about this?" Sigrid showed the court the paper she had taken from Morgan's desk. "See? Morgan himself named his killer!"

"Perhaps our late king was only writing Fleydur's name to announce His Majesty's heir. King Morgan did say he'd start on his will tonight," said the general.

"Tell me, then, why is the paper bloodstained?" Sigrid raised the sheet high for all to see.

Birds murmured, frowning.

"And you promised," whispered Sigrid to Fleydur. She turned to the court. "Check his words! You all heard him promise he wouldn't break his father's heart." Sigrid placed a set of talons upon her own chest. "But now our king's heart is broken, utterly broken." Her words turned into sobs.

"Let us vote. Is Fleydur guilty of the two crimes, yea or nay?" said Amicus. He turned to the bronze scales. "O founder eagle of our mountain, who sees truth and falsehood alike, show us which direction now the Skythunder tribe is to fly."

Fleydur had known he would hear those words again. But, instead of an assembly to vote on his dream of a music school, there was an assembly to try him for atrocities committed against his own father!

He lifted his eyes toward the bronze eagle of the balance. The eagle that had seemed so kindly to him before this now stared emptily ahead. The advisers placed their voting stones on the scale.

How the bronze eagle groaned, tilting far to one side, as if it had been stabbed in the back. Fleydur listened to the staccato of yeas.

Ten yeas. Five nays.

Then Forlath, holding the king's three-vote stone, chose nay, but it was no use: with his vote it was still ten to eight. The vote was close—yet this time, the king's stone did not shift the balance.

"Prince Fleydur," boomed the secretary. "The Iron Nest has found you guilty."

"An eye for an eye, a feather for a feather, a death for a death!" the Iron Nest chanted.

Sigrid flung the black veil from her face. "Nothing less than death!" she agreed. The shouts grew to a feverish pitch, nearly drowning out Forlath's voice:

"No!"

Sigrid glared at Forlath, who was gripping Morgan's scepter tightly.

Forlath did not look at Fleydur. "Father's funeral must be attended to first—that is the law. You cannot tarnish a king's burial with the death of a criminal. The execution will be postponed." He struck the ground with his scepter, his face a cold mask. "Till then, throw him into the dungeon!"

It had been generations since the dungeon had been inhabited, years since it was last opened. Many did not know what it looked like, so they crept to the padlocked entrance and watched the guards oil the rusted locks and push open the creaking, heavy iron door. A foul wind of mildew and rot blew out.

Fleydur glanced back once, as the two guards steered him down into the dark mouth of the dungeon. His heart tore against his ribs. Never had he imagined anybird accusing him of killing his father. He had done nothing! No, he corrected himself. He *had* done something. He had returned home when nobird wanted him to.

Hurry, scurry, work and worry: helter-skelter,
hurly-burly.
—FROM THE *BOOK OF HERESY*

22
HURRYING

It is done," Tranglarhad said, slamming the iron door behind him. Silence filled the vast space in the Castle of Earth, for all the owls there knew what he meant. Tranglarhad hurried toward his laboratory in the depth of the caverns. There, Kawaka stood up, angry. "Finally you return!"

"What ails you?" said the owl.

"While you were on the mountaintop, enjoying

playing teacher, I went off to recruit other archaeopteryxes. It was hard enough for me to sneak a band into Sword Mountain unnoticed. When I brought my recruits to your door, your underlings refused to let them in! What's the meaning of this?"

"Did they? It must have been a misunderstanding," Tranglarhad replied, although it was he who had given this order. The owl had worried that while he was away Kawaka would gather forces to usurp his Castle of Earth.

"There isn't anyplace else to hide such a large group of soldiers," continued Kawaka. "I had to remove them and house them just outside the mountain range. Many of them got fed up and deserted. Now only a few dozen remain." Kawaka pounded the table. "And you stand there nodding your big head, doing nothing."

"Excuse me?" Tranglarhad shouted, incensed. "I have accomplished what I said I would do; I have the gemstone right now, and have snapped the wings of the eagle kingdom!" The owl wrenched the Leasorn gem out of his pocket and flashed its purple light into Kawaka's eyes.

Surprised, Kawaka forgot his anger. "I cannot believe it! No army's chased you down?"

"That's because the king is dead."

"Such great timing!" the archaeopteryx exclaimed admiringly.

"Why, thank you. I wish I could have stayed to watch, indeed."

"I have never met a bird like you." Kawaka shook his head. He extended a claw. "Since that's all finished, give me back the *Book of Heresy*!"

"Not so fast," said Tranglarhad.

"I have to have it! It bears my former emperor Maldeor's script. It will help me recruit more soldiers, in the name of the empire."

"I need it for tonight," said Tranglarhad.

"I need it more! If what you said about the eagle king is all true, then now is the time to attack them. They are at their most vulnerable. Why do you delay?"

"Upon my pellet, have I not already expressed to you my profound indifference to the blood and guts of battle?" the owl said calmly. "I have gotten what I wanted—the Leasorn gemstone. And I need the *Book of Heresy* for a little longer."

"What for?" Kawaka's face darkened.

"Your emperor was very interested in this type of gem and I intend to use the Leasorn to make sunglass lenses," said Tranglarhad. "In owl legend, if an owl wears sunglasses made of a magical stone, he will gain the sight of day. And when he takes them off, he retains it forever. The *Book of Heresy* will verify whether the Leasorn is the stone that I need. Then, I will be as powerful as the eagles; no, more so. I will be a bird of both worlds, of both night and day!"

"You can keep the book a little longer," consented Kawaka. "But I will bring my recruits here, and this time you will let them in." *And you will give the gemstone, too, I'll see to that!* he added silently.

Tranglarhad started to fill his alchemists' furnace with coals. "Leave, then," he said. But as soon as Kawaka departed, he motioned to one of his owls. "Some effort it took to pry the archaeopteryx from this book! Hide it in a cliff for safekeeping till this evening's work is done."

As the other owl flew off, Tranglarhad coaxed the flames inside the furnace. He trod up and down on the bellows pedals. "It will take a while to reach the desired heat," he said to his owls. "Meanwhile, let the party begin!"

Never had Dandelion left Sword Mountain and flown so far.

She beat against the wind through snow, hoping she would be able to find Cloud-wing at Double Pain Peak. As she kept low to escape the worst of the wind, the snowfall intensified, whole chunks hitting her in the face and clattering on her wings.

She glanced about for stars to get her bearings, but the eyes of the sky were closed to her. Her face upturned, Dandelion was caught unawares by a strong gust of wind. Her wings buckled. The next thing she knew, tree branches cut her cheek and she was tossed into a snowdrift. She could not see anything.

Dandelion waited to catch her breath. She was snugly curled within the snow as if within an eggshell.

The raging of the wind outside was muted. A voice in her mind said to her, *You should have planned better.*

Dandelion tried to move, but the voice told her, *Just rest now. See, it's so calm here. It'll soon get comfortable. And you won't have to worry anymore about the world outside.*

Dandelion shook the words from her mind. She raised her talons and pounded the snow, trying to find a place to break free.

Why don't you stay here? the voice said, louder. *You've lost your crown. You are an orphan again. You're released from responsibility.*

Angered by the words, Dandelion clawed to break free of the ice shell. As she emerged, she stood wobbling on her feet, panting.

She didn't have a crown anymore, but that did not mean she hadn't learned a thing or two about the responsibilities of a princess. Princess or not, she would stand up for those around her. Princess or not, she would not perch aside, watching injustice slip past, without doing everything in her power to right it. And princess or not, she would not be afraid to do what it takes to stand against it.

The wind lessened, and Dandelion spied the stars again. She continued on her flight. A grim shape soon loomed on the horizon, a fort built of stone over a steep drop. When she folded her wings to land outside the front door, something jabbed like daggers into her sides. Icicles had formed along her feathers.

"Young lass, what are you doing here? Go back to your fireplace!" said the school's gatekeeper. He muttered further when he heard that she needed to see Cloud-wing. Dandelion wanted to shout with exasperation.

"Prince Fleydur has been arrested for a crime he did not commit. I think Cloud-wing can help me prove Fleydur's innocence," she said.

Dandelion was allowed in. She waited in the corridor, shaking the ice from her wings.

"Dandelion?" Cloud-wing said, astounded, as he flew over.

Dandelion jumped right into her news. "Fleydur's in trouble! He's been accused of killing King Morgan *and* stealing the Leasorn gem."

"Great Spirit!" shouted Cloud-wing. Other eagles crept from their dormitory, listening. "He couldn't have done that."

Dandelion lowered her voice. "The tutor is the thief. That owl, Tranglarhad. He's fled."

"He called himself an expert on stones," Cloud-wing said, remembering Pudding describing his father's conference with the owl. "Do you know where he's gone?"

"Well, he warned about poisonous fumes, too," reminded Dandelion. "He warned birds away from the mine."

"It makes sense if he lives there," Cloud-wing said, his eyes lighting up.

"Tranglarhad talked about living *below* here. Not in the valley, he said. Birds thought he meant below the summit, but I think he means beneath the mountain rock itself. Cloud-wing, haven't you visited the old mine? Do you remember where the entrance is?"

Cloud-wing nodded. He understood at once what Dandelion was proposing. He quickly assembled four birds to accompany them.

Isobello was a small peregrine falcon, with the

quickness and agility to slip through holes and cracks and scout ahead. With Pandey the osprey's strong sense of direction, they would not get easily lost. Blitz and Blaze, golden eagle twins, had a sense of humor but were also serious fighters.

They gathered matches and a lantern, and tip-clawed to the armory. By the light of the lantern, they donned leather armor and armed themselves thoroughly. Dandelion kept the sword that Fleydur had given her. Cloud-wing found his claymore, Pandey selected a spear, Isobello a sling, and Blitz and Blaze, broadswords.

"This is our test, Rockbottom raptors," said Cloud-wing, with a nod at Dandelion to include her as well.

"Wheeeeee. Ka-boom!" they exclaimed in unison.

"Follow me," said Cloud-wing. "There are fewer guards at the back of the school. We'll be able to sneak out from there." Soon Double Pain Peak was a blur in the night sky behind them.

The bowels of the mountain rumble—the truth shall emerge!
—from the *Book of Heresy*

23
THE CASTLE OF EARTH

The six young raptors banked and descended toward the foothills of Sword Mountain, Cloud-wing guiding them toward the sinister-looking gray boulders that hid the entrance of the mine.

There appeared to be no signs of life, no wink of light anywhere. But Cloud-wing laid his talons against one side of the hollow, moving slowly into a narrow cave. "Here's a gap," said Cloud-wing, gesturing at a crack in the wall. "I don't think the boulders are packed so tightly beyond this part." They all paused, unsure. Then, with a reckless abandon, they raced forward, squeezed in their bellies, and flattened their wings tight to their sides. An adult eagle would not have fit into this hole.

"Good thing none of us were at the king's feast to stuff ourselves," Blaze joked.

"Or we'd be stuck here for sure," Blitz said.

As they helped one another slip through to the other side, Dandelion struck a match and lit their lantern. It illumined how precariously the boulders were balanced around them. A fist-sized rock suddenly fell onto the ground. A shower of pebbles and dust followed. They heard other parts of the cave awakening.

"Let's hurry," she said, feeling caged.

Cloud-wing was right; there was more room here. As if they were picking a path in a maze, they stepped gingerly. Dandelion was afraid that they might not be able to find their way back, so she paused, unpinned one of the five gold acorns on her collar, and dropped it behind her to mark the right path. After they came across a place where the cave branched off in several directions, she dropped another one.

The air was filled with stone dust motes. Creatures scurried away underfoot. At length, they made out the gaping black mouth of the ancient mine. Though they had worried that they would not find it, the sight of its crumbling green-tinged bricks brought hesitation, not joy.

"Tranglarhad and his bunch—they're really down there, aren't they?" Isobello asked Cloud-wing. All of them shuddered.

"Since this side's pretty much blocked off, I don't believe the owls would stay close to the entrance," ventured Cloud-wing, and so they stepped into the mine. Preferring to have the certainty of ground under their talons, they started out on foot.

The darkness swirled around them in unseen fantastical shapes, but by the feeble glow of the lantern hanging from Dandelion's beak, they discovered a direct path to the mine's main tunnel. They trudged on, stepping on fragile stone chips. As the birds went deeper, the chips piled up higher. They were very small elongated or angular shapes, and gleamed pale yellow under the lantern light.

"I've a feeling these bits will reach up and block off the tunnel," said Pandey. "Should we turn back? Maybe there's a side shaft."

"Do you hear something?" said Dandelion through a clenched beak.

They heard a rumbling behind them, and dull thuds on the ground as if there was a herd of stampeding animals chasing them.

"The mine's blocked," said Pandey, his voice choked with panic. "Our entryway's been sealed!" Their breath caught in their throats, and they stopped moving.

"Then our only way is to go on," said Cloud-wing.

The low ceiling ruled out any possibility of flight. They pushed on, trying to focus on what was ahead of them. Soon they found themselves wading chest deep in the jumble of fine white chips. They struggled to lift each talon through the shifting fragments, moving in slow motion. Each centimeter forward was a victory. The smaller bits found their way into the birds' feathers, digging sharply against their bare skin.

The farther they went, the more evident it became that not all of the chips were dry, smooth, and light. The ones buried down around their feet felt hairy, even squishy.

"What is this stuff, anyway?" said Isobello at last in a trembling voice, asking the question that all of them had been thinking for some time.

Dandelion scooped up the top layer of it with a wing. There was a fine dust mingled with the chips. She looked about. They were piled in gentle dunes, as far as the lantern light could show her.

"Does it give off poisonous gas? It doesn't smell right," said Pandey. "I don't know."

"It's not chalk or any sort of rock," said Cloud-wing.

Dandelion nearly gagged when she realized the truth. "Owl pellets!" she croaked as she set the lantern on the ground. "Thousands and thousands of owl pellets!"

They were wading through an ocean of shattered bones. The revelation made them all quake. Rodent bones, that was what those white chips were: little fractured skulls and ribs and limbs. The squishy hairy masses were pellets that had not yet decomposed. How many owls must live in the bowels of the mines to regurgitate all these?

"Great Spirit!" groaned Pandey while the twins, Blitz and Blaze, made retching sounds.

The owls don't live near here, of course, thought Dandelion. *But that doesn't mean they don't use the place—the garbage is a sure line of defense against unwelcome intruders.*

Isobello, the smallest and shortest among them, struggled as the bones gradually rose to the level of his neck. "I'm going to be buried!" he said, gasping for breath. "What if we get stuck here and become part of these bones?" Cloud-wing made his way to the falcon and helped him along. "You lead with the lantern," he said to Dandelion. They struggled on, deeply shaken, without speaking another word, until Cloud-wing cried, "Do you hear voices?"

They cocked their heads. Frenzied, off-key chants echoed in the tunnel. "Look!" Dandelion said. "There's a patch of light over there!"

Turning to a widened tunnel to their left, they saw a huge patch of eerie, shifting light.

After a moment of hesitation, they changed their direction and moved slowly toward it. They worked through the tallest dune yet, emerging on the other side with a shower of the garbage, and the discovery that the drifts of pellets diminished here. Soon they were on a stretch of rock again.

A part of the tunnel floor had collapsed into a natural cavern below, and it was from this cavern that the firelight and the singing came. Smoke rose to sting their nostrils.

Silently the young raptors crept toward the jagged edge of the hole, flattened themselves on the cold stone, and peered down.

It was an underground celebration, twenty feet below. A crackling fire dominated the scene, roasting kabobs of meat. Around its flames danced a dozen eagle owls, kicking and prancing in a conga line. They flung out their wings toward the fire in time to a drum, sidling up close to the bright flames and skipping back. All of them wore dark glasses. Their beaks were curled in maniacal glee as they chanted:

> *To a proper owl*
> *No accessory surpasses*
> *Two glinting shields of crystal—*
> *A pair of sunglasses!*
>
> *They tone down all that's bright*
> *So we'll fly out in the day.*
> *All shines as clear as night—*
> *No more limits in our way!*
>
> *One for you, and one for me.*
> *Remember, keep your cool!*
> *They'll see how wise are we.*
> *And after all, who'd dare to call—*
> *A bespectacled owl a fool?*

Other owls swaying in the shadows hooted in pleasure, raising wineglasses the size of fruit bowls in toasts at each stanza.

"Here you have it, the ultimate masterpiece of cunning: The king dead, the gem filched, the kingdom split, and still enough time for some jolly partying at day's end. To the folly of the hookbeaks upstairs! May it last indefinitely," declared one owl as he burped loudly. The others cheered.

"Show us the prize. Show us the gemstone!" they shouted. They were calling to an unseen figure in an adjacent cavern.

"It's Tranglarhad!" Dandelion whispered.

Indeed, the former tutor appeared below the eagles, making modest gestures to calm the cheering crowd. "Since my friend Kawaka has departed from our castle, I have examined the stone carefully under a magnifying glass, and I must declare that it is what we have sought— the material to craft the best of sunglasses." He displayed a deep purple stone to the onlookers. "It is as our 'Chant of Sunglasses' says: 'We'll fly out in the day!'"

Where was the scholarly dress of the tutor now? The true appearance of their teacher was revealed: twisted face mounted by dark glasses to keep off the glare of the fire, studded belt cinching a dirty coat, two gleaming square cleavers tucked one on each side.

Directly above, the young birds looked anxiously at one another.

"How many glasses will the stone yield?" asked one owl.

"Used sparingly, five pairs," mused Tranglarhad. "And maybe some left over for a monocle. By the time the party is over, the furnace will have reached the correct heat for the final melting to begin!"

Dandelion realized that to retrieve the gem, and to find another way out, they would have to defeat the gathered mass below. Most of the owls did not appear to have weapons, yet they looked tough and dangerous, even with only wineglasses in their talons.

Tranglarhad clasped the gemstone with a pair of tongs. "See how it reveals the dark side of light!" he exclaimed as he lifted it skyward. His gaze rose with the gem.

And Cloud-wing dived, thrusting his claymore, reaching for the upraised gem.

"Wha—?" Tranglarhad shouted. Before Cloud-wing could get close, the tongs dropped out of the owl's claws. The gem skittered across the floor, blocked from sight by other owls fluttering toward Cloud-wing. Before their advantage of surprise wore off, Dandelion and the eagles attacked, shrieking raptor cries.

"Upon my pellet, the blasted gem! Conjured up hookbeaks from the bones in our garbage dump, it did."

Gargling curses, Tranglarhad leaped up high, swinging a cleaver at Cloud-wing's head.

Dandelion tore off a gold acorn from her collar and hurled it toward Tranglarhad just as he hacked. The heavy pin hit Tranglarhad's sunglasses, shattering one of the lenses and distracting him so that Cloud-wing could dodge away. Dandelion saw that broken glass had bloodied the owl's face. Tranglarhad blinked through the empty frame and screeched.

"Are you all right?" Dandelion cried to Cloud-wing.

"Yes," he said. "Thanks."

"The princess, is it?" said the owl, enraged. "Little weed! But sharp eyes and ears won't save your life." He spun around and sliced down with his other cleaver. Dandelion pulled out Wind-voice's sword from her belt and met his lunge. Tranglarhad growled.

"You thief! And you lectured us against stealing!" Dandelion yelled.

"The classroom is not the world," the owl returned.

Just then, one of Tranglarhad's minions called out, "High Owl, that filthy hookbeak's got the gem!"

Tranglarhad spun around, joining the rest of the owls as they crowded around Pandey, who had dived under the mob of owls to snatch the Leasorn gem from the floor.

"Catch!" shouted the osprey, frantic. He flung the

gemstone over the owls' heads. Cloud-wing caught it and the owls surged toward him. The young raptors flew out of the cavern into a tunnel, trying to distance themselves from their enemies.

"You think you can steal from me, the master thief? You aren't going anywhere," hollered Tranglarhad. "This labyrinth has you trapped."

"Keep going, hurry!" said Cloud-wing. "Don't panic. There must be another exit in these caverns—one that the owls use. There must be another way out!"

They followed tunnel after tunnel, breathing hard. Then, in front of them, they saw a gate. They could hear sounds of wind and falling water just beyond. This was the owls' main door. It was ajar.

They strained their wings, the owls pursuing, others swooping in from side tunnels. Cloud-wing, using the glowing gemstone to light their way, sped toward the gate. Just as he was about to pull open the door, it flung wide of its own accord. An archaeopteryx entered, wielding a torch in one foot, a cutlass in the other. Kawaka gave a rattling cry and attacked Cloud-wing with his torch as three more archaeopteryxes poured in, blocking the only exit.

"We've got you now!" said Tranglarhad from behind.

Where shall you flee the flame of my fury?
—FROM THE *BOOK OF HERESY*

24
CONSUMED

Cloud-wing cried out sharply as Kawaka's torch blazed in his face but managed to rejoin the group. They swung around, not knowing where they were going. At the first side tunnel, they turned and flew.

"The laboratory!" Tranglarhad was screaming in glee. "They're heading for the laboratory. Quick, quick! Go around them, cut them off!"

With no more side tunnels along the way, they were forced to fly straight on, toward someplace that seemed hotter and hotter, as if the lava from the center of the earth bubbled to the surface there. Bursting into a large cavern, they saw that owls had already taken other shortcuts and poured in from other doors.

Dandelion glanced back, recognizing with terror Kawaka's disfigured beak. The archaeopteryx was gaining on them speedily. In the heat, Kawaka's shout of triumph seemed to crack their eardrums. There was no place to fly anymore. Cloud-wing, the last in their group, lost his balance and tumbled in the air. Kawaka overcame him, knocked away his claymore, and snatched up the gemstone. Five owls surrounded Cloud-wing immediately and caught hold of his wings.

Tranglarhad entered the laboratory. "Don't you dare move. Drop your weapons!" he warned Dandelion and the academy students. He pointed at Cloud-wing, writhing in the clutches of his captors. "Or he gets killed."

Tranglarhad raised a cleaver to Cloud-wing's throat.

"No matter what, we'll all stay together, Cloud-wing," whispered Dandelion.

All fell silent except the alchemist's furnace, a glowing monster in the middle of the laboratory that sputtered and spat metallic heat. From behind its latched mouth, flames clawed. Dandelion, Blitz and Blaze, Pandey, and Isobello surrendered. The owls tossed their weapons into a pile in a corner, then wrenched their wings and held them tight.

Cloud-wing stared wide-eyed at them as Tranglarhad pressed the cleaver closer to his throat. Slowly, a drop of blood, then another, rolled down along the silver edge of the blade. It was then that Dandelion noticed something different about Cloud-wing's eyes. Fresh scorch marks charred the feathers near them. He was blinking as if he was having trouble seeing.

"Why not just slay them all?" growled Kawaka, tossing the gemstone from one set of claws to the other.

"They'll be useful," said Tranglarhad. "With a top-notch catch like this, some royalty and nobility, we might gain whatever we want without bloodshed. Eagles will relinquish anything rather than let their little ones be hurt. But anyhow—" Tranglarhad abruptly left Cloud-wing, motioning to two other owls to guard him. Cloud-wing shuddered and drooped, clutching his throat. The other owls squinted, keeping a respectful distance from the furnace as Tranglarhad went forward and threw open the hatch.

"We have secured the gemstone. The party's spoiled, but the furnace is ready. Give the Leasorn gem to me!"

He held out a claw toward Kawaka.

Kawaka did not move. The other archaeopteryxes, twenty or so, flanked their leader. "The stone," he said, "is property of the archaeopteryx empire."

Tranglarhad blinked. "What did you say?"

"You heard me."

"But—but it's rightfully mine!" shouted Tranglarhad. "I risked my ear tufts on the mountaintop to get it."

Kawaka stowed the gemstone inside his uniform. "And I might return it to you—if you return the *Book of Heresy* first!"

Tranglarhad watched Kawaka's recruits. One was lazily eyeing the laboratory's tools and furnishings, gauging their value. Another was whetting a sword upon a stalagmite, whistling as if at home. The High Owl knew he should not have let Kawaka bring his troops in. *But if I give up the book now, I have nothing, nothing but an armed troop inside my own lair*, Tranglarhad thought. The owl stood firm. "No, you give me the gem first."

"No, you the book."

"You!"

Kawaka raised his cutlass in reply.

Every pair of eyes was now on him and Tranglarhad. The grasp of the owls on Dandelion and the academy students loosened.

Dandelion seized the chance. A desperate idea had formed in her mind. "The gemstone's magical! If you tell it to sing your heart, it will reveal its new owner."

"Did you teach your students such nonsense?" Kawaka said derisively. "Sentimentality!" He cackled. "'Sing my heart' all right . . ."

Before he finished his sentence, the gem inside his uniform rang with a deep note. He looked down, shocked.

"Sing *my* heart," spat Tranglarhad. A different tune rose from the gem, discordant with the first, and louder. He waved his claws at his minions. They hooted the same, joined by the roars of the archaeopteryxes. The cacophony was so horrendous that Kawaka dropped his cutlass to cover his ears.

Taking his chance, Tranglarhad leaped at Kawaka and sliced Kawaka's uniform open with a flick of one blade.

Catching the loud gem that spilled out, the owl turned to the furnace, grimacing as the sound rose higher and higher, harsher and harsher, the notes of the owls clashing and grating against the tunes of the archae-opteryxes. As Tranglarhad fumbled to place the gem inside, Kawaka rushed behind him and kicked.

His foot had barely grazed the owl's tailfeathers when

the gem touched the coals. As if to mirror the owls' shock and despair, the gem distilled from its jarring repertoire one loud, pure high note. The furnace vibrated, cracked, and exploded, spewing flames and the noise of true chaos. Shards of iron shot through the air. Tranglarhad was blown backward. The glass vials along the walls burst from the heat, releasing horrid odors. Thick black fumes rolled and filled the laboratory. The owls holding the young raptors captive broke away, dashing toward Tranglarhad, who was obscured in the smoke.

Kawaka choked. His skin burned from all the debris that had shot under his feathers, and for a moment he could barely stand. He rallied his soldiers to hunt for Tranglarhad as well. The archaeopteryxes and the owls began battling, but the owls were too scattered to sustain a strong front.

Confused and disoriented, none of them saw that the gemstone had burst out of the furnace along with the debris. An owl tripped over it, sending it rolling toward Dandelion.

Dandelion kept low and grabbed the Leasorn gem, then doubled back toward the corner where her sword was piled with her friends' weapons. She threw a gold acorn pin at an owl who tried to stop her, stunning him with a hit right between the eyes.

Despite his wounds, Cloud-wing was already beside her, snatching up his claymore.

"Where? Where to?" groaned Isobello. Their ears still rang from the loudness. They dashed back toward the way they'd come, hoping to reach the door with the sound of a waterfall behind it, but the archaeopteryxes had already blocked the exit. There was only one shabby door on the other side that was nearer to them than any enemy.

"This is your last chance to escape!" Cloud-wing called out raggedly to them.

Your? Dandelion thought. Just then, Kawaka broke free from a bunch of owls.

"The Leasorn gem! Has it been shattered?" he demanded.

He saw Dandelion holding it and gestured to his archaeoptcryxes. "Seize them."

"Go. Go on without me," Cloud-wing urged. "I can hardly see to fly—but I can cover you. I'll distract them!"

This time you're wrong, Cloud-wing, Dandelion thought.

She yanked out her rope and crammed one end into Cloud-wing's claws.

"Just hold on," she said before he could protest.

As Kawaka's recruits hurled themselves at the young

birds, Dandelion and her friends flew through the door and plunged into the darkness, leaving the chaos and battle behind them.

Fear choked them; they felt the weight of Sword Mountain pressing down from above. Only the lavender glow from the Leasorn gem lighted their dark path. The rope strained in Dandelion's claws, and she held tight; with Cloud-wing at the other end, she would never let go. Echoes of their wing beats bounced off the stalactites that stabbed down like stone daggers. The caverns stretched before them, bigger than they had anticipated. It was like a castle unto itself—a Castle of Earth. They made so much noise, weaving through the tunnels, that the archaeopteryxes found their trail easily.

They fled down a narrow and dirty stretch of caves, smelling foul and dusty—nobird, not even the slovenly owls, had inhabited this section for a long time.

Suddenly, a dead end forced them to halt. Trapped. Nothing but stone all around.

They stalled, looking about desperately. "Up!" cried Dandelion. "There's a break in the ceiling!"

It resembled a smoke shaft. It was not in the direction they'd hoped for; it led farther, deeper into the heart of the mountain, but they flew toward it, grasping at any chance. Blitz and Blaze slashed at spiderwebs from its opening, and they rose frantically into the darkness, one after another.

The archaeopteryxes arrived at the dead end and froze, gazing up into the shaft, into territory where not even the bravest of owls had ever ventured.

"Fools!" Kawaka said. "That crack was made by an earthquake. They'll either have to turn back, or get stuck up there and die."

"Do you want us to wait it out?" asked an archaeopteryx.

"No—we'll smoke them out with these torches and speed up the process," ordered Kawaka. "Their bodies will drop back down here, or the gem—whichever falls first!"

Up in the shaft, Dandelion and her friends fluttered blindly, their wingtips slapping the walls. They were in the throat of the mountain, at its mercy. What was above them? Dandelion glanced up once and saw nothing but walls of stone that seemed to lean in and merge into a flat plane of darkness. They heard the screeches and the cries of the archaeopteryxes shouting up at them. But gradually they became more distant, and the orange glow of the torches below became no more than a pinprick of light. Then that, too, was gone as the shaft twisted, and there was darkness all around. The shaft narrowed with each passing second, and they were forced to fly closer together. The smoke from the archaeopteryxes's torches wound itself around their bodies, stinging their eyes and throats as they panted in the heat.

Tapping the edges of the tunnel with her talons, Dandelion unexpectedly felt a side shaft branching off in a horizontal direction. She illuminated the opening with the gemstone, and encouraging one another, the birds ventured down this new direction, crawling speedily.

"Oh, no!" she said. "Stop."

"What?"

"Turn back. The tunnel's narrowed off," she explained, finding that she could only fit her talons in the crack ahead of her.

They shuffled and stumbled back to the vertical shaft. It was not to be the first time. Again and again they encountered side shafts, but they always found that the tunnel tapered to a gap too narrow to squeeze through. Each time the disappointment burned still deeper. They'd rest in the nooks, not daring to speak, before turning back to the main shaft.

Our breathing sounds so loud, Dandelion thought time after time. Their swallows, gulps, sniffs revealed just how frightened and vulnerable they actually were.

They dismissed these thoughts and continued to

follow the main shaft in its unending upward spiral. Feathers bent and snapped in the tight space. Their wings would give way at some point soon and—then what? They had struggled all this way for nothing? Only to fall, little sad bundles of feathers, one hitting another, right down to despair and death in the waiting ring of archaeopteryxes?

Why are we still moving? Why do we keep flying up? Dandelion thought. *Nobird's chasing us now.* And yet: They were trying to distance themselves from panic. They must keep moving, constantly moving, to stay ahead of its grasp.

Their strength was waning. Time and time again, one slipped and faltered, crashing onto the bird below, generating a moment of tight confusion. "Hurry! Hurry!" moaned the birds lower down the line.

"It's so dark," Cloud-wing said, gritting his beak.

Dandelion held the gemstone toward him. "Some light," she said. Its lavender glow showed the dark spot of blood growing at his throat.

The shaft cramped them in further till they could not stretch their wings. They arched their backs and extended their legs, bracing themselves in the narrow space. Their claws scrabbled to find purchase. Still they climbed upward, much slower now, the weapons strapped to their bodies scraping against rock.

Soreness throbbed in their shoulders and wings. Tension pounded their backs and legs. At last they could no longer move up without wobbling and risking a fall.

Finally they consented to rest and paused and listened to the silence, and here panic caught up with them. The very air they breathed seemed to get scarcer and scarcer. Their lungs labored, their beaks opened wide.

They vowed hurriedly to one another that they would catch anybird, should one of them slip. Then they waited—for what, they dared not think.

Holding the gem in her beak, Dandelion tore a strip of cloth from her hem and tried to staunch the bleeding on Cloud-wing's throat. She used another strip to bind the makeshift bandage into place but found the piece was too short to tie a knot. She took off her last acorn pin and used it to secure the bandage.

"Can you see better?" she said, moving the gem closer.

Cloud-wing was still holding the rope—the rope that he had used to teach her to fly, long ago.

"I'll be here, at the other end of the rope, and I'll hold you up. . . ."

He pressed it back into Dandelion's grasp as he lifted his face toward her.

She saw something glistening slide down his cheek. "Yes, Dandelion," he whispered.

"How long have we been underground, you think?" she said.

Cloud-wing considered. "Five hours? I can't tell." He looked toward their other companions.

"More than that, surely," said Blitz. "You think it's morning outside?"

"We'll never know, will we?" said Isobello.

They panted, drawing ragged breaths. The thought of slow suffocation sent a spear of dread into Dandelion's heart, and the purple glowing gemstone in her talons was the only comfort.

"Great Spirit. This place is like a coffin!" said Pandey.

Nobird had the heart to reply.

Laughing at a funeral? Occasionally it is apt.
—FROM THE *BOOK OF HERESY*

25
FUNERAL

Fleydur raised his head and saw Forlath descending from the dungeon stairs, his black mourning cloak sweeping down each step.

"It's morning. Unbelievable, isn't it? First morning without Father," Forlath said. Shaking his head, he drifted closer, till he nearly leaned against the iron bars. "I know you are innocent, Fleydur, but with Father dead, everybird is lost in grief, and nobird has reason anymore."

"I know you will do the best for the mountain," answered Fleydur.

"I will try. The eagles, especially my mother and the Iron Nest, want a scapegoat for their anguish. In truth, you are safest here for now, away from them. I must leave to attend the funeral, but I will get you out somehow!" Forlath's face trembled. A set of his talons curled around the iron bars.

Fleydur reached out to touch his brother. "Forlath..."

His chains clinked. It sounded like a ghastly echo of the bells Fleydur had worn when he first returned.

Forlath clasped Fleydur's talons through the bars for a moment before he left.

The frost of daybreak glistened on the windows. The eagles who had celebrated Morgan's birthday became the attendants of his funeral. A flood of birds dressed in black assembled in the main hall. Morgan's coffin now rested in the central spot where the magnificent mountain cake had stood. With anguish, the mourners recalled the tutor's wish: *"Good health and long life."*

They lined themselves up, holding hats and flowers, waiting to have a last look at their beloved king. Their eyes lingered upon his face. In death, Morgan seemed to have shrunk beneath his feathers.

When the last golden eagle had paid his respects, the coffin lid was lowered. The eagles burst into wild, despairing cries. Outside, the gong beat madly, passionately, without rhythm or order.

Ten guards lifted the coffin and flew out of the castle, flying high up in the air, slowly circling the mountaintop one last time—the death flight of Morgan. And all across the mountain range, eagles stopped what they were doing, turned in the direction of Sword Mountain, and wailed, "No! No! No!" The valleys echoed with their cries, and the mountain itself seemed to shift and rock in mourning for the king.

On foot, the eagles began the descent toward the final resting place where the stone coffins of the kings hung from cliffs.

"O king!" cried the funeral chanter at the head of the procession. "Where are you now?"

"Not here!" sobbed the eagles of the funeral procession.

"O king! You led us well, through crisis and war. Where are you now?"

"Not here!" moaned the generals, the advisers.

"O king! Your soul rises in the sky to paint it a brighter blue. Where are you now?"

Sigrid tore at her veil. "Not here!" she wailed.

The chanter flung her wings to the sky. "We miss you! We miss the sunshine of your kindly face. Come back."

"Come back!" cried the eagles.

"We are orphans, every one of us!"

"Come back!" cried the eagles.

"We miss you. Every one of us begs you, O king! Where are you n—"

"Argh!" There was banging; then the coffin lid flew open. The wind blew the shroud off Morgan's face. The corpse struggled to sit up, incoherent gargling coming from his throat.

The pallbearers' legs buckled.

"Great Spirit!" exclaimed the funeral chanter. "Nobird actually came *back* before!" The chanter fled from the funeral train, frightened out of her wits.

Morgan coughed out a golden granule in a gush of black blood. "Who's calling me? I am here," he rasped, staring at the eagles with bloodshot eyes.

It was so quiet the mourners could hear the chains of the suspended coffins creaking on the vertical graveyard cliff.

"It's really too cold, close the window. Goodness! What are you doing in that awful black garb? Who has died?" the delirious king demanded. The eagles closest to the coffin leaned in, astounded.

"Y-you have . . . I mean, we thought you had d-d-died," one stuttered.

"Outrageous! And right on my birthday! Do I look dead to you?" Morgan gripped the sides of the coffin and tried to clamber out. He was too weak. Giving up, he sat straight, as stately as if on his throne, wrapping the shroud tightly around his shoulders to ward off the chill.

The onlookers got over their initial shock and cheered, flinging the funeral wreaths and bouquets high into the air.

The court physician hurried over to Morgan. "Are you all right now, Your Majesty?"

Morgan nodded. "Better." He studied one face after another. "All of you who should be at my funeral are here, except . . . Where is Fleydur?" he said.

"He could not be here," said the queen.

"He hasn't left me again, has he?"

"No. He's locked in the dungeon," said a member of the Iron Nest.

"What for?"

"He promised not to break your heart," said Sigrid. "But he did—he took a treasure of the kingdom. And we thought . . . I thought . . ."

Morgan slapped the side panel of the coffin. "What do you mean? Summon him to me at once!"

The weight of justice cannot be ignored.
—FROM THE OLD SCRIPTURE

26
THE BRONZE SCALES

Tranglarhad the owl, singed by fire and mortally injured by debris, opened his orange eyes as he lay in the rubble of his laboratory. Smoke, like ghosts of glory, lingered before his eyes.

It was wrong of me to try to warp myself into a creature of day, he thought. "I do not belong to the light," he said to himself.

"But I demand a dignity for those who live in the

dark!" He shook a balled set of talons at the stalactites. The owl breathed heavily and thought that the whole mountain pressed down on his chest. "Go chase those archaeopteryxes! Drive them out of here!" he croaked to his followers.

"What about you, High Owl?"

Tranglarhad fell back. "I dream," he said, his voice fading. "In my unending darkness, I have unending dreams."

Hooting for revenge, the leaderless owls regrouped and cornered Kawaka as he had cornered Dandelion and her friends. The archaeopteryx fought off the tangle of owls. He would come back to tame these fools later. The young raptors did not seem likely to return anytime soon, so Kawaka would need to go up into the shaft himself, kill them, and retrieve the gemstone.

He summoned his troops and rushed up the shaft. Kawaka raised his cutlass in front, prepared to spike any eagles trapped above him.

Several hundreds of feet above, Dandelion, Cloud-wing, and their friends shivered, wedged in the narrow crack. From time to time they halfheartedly scooted up a few more inches.

In the light of the Leasorn gemstone, Dandelion watched a quivering smudge farther up. It drifted down slowly, showing itself to be a moth. She nudged Cloud-wing. He rubbed his eye slowly, trying to see.

The moth bumbled from wall to wall. Six pairs of eyes watched its progress silently.

"Any of you want to eat it?" said Blitz, who was below Cloud-wing. "It's coming near my talons."

Pandey snorted. "The only worse thing than being trapped in a crack is being trapped in a crack with a fluttering in your throat."

"Tickles of death," said Blaze.

Their chuckles were rudely interrupted.

"Hark! I hear them!" Kawaka's voice boomed loud in the narrow space. "I think I see the gem!"

The group moaned and scrambled frantically upward.

"It's no use. No matter how far we'll go, we're trapped," groaned Pandey. They hurried, they groped, and the shaft grew narrower, narrower.

"We can stop," declared Cloud-wing. "We'll just fight to the death!" Kawaka's ragged panting was closer, closer. They imagined that his breath stirred their feathers.

"Great Spirit!" shouted Dandelion as if waking from a dream. "Where you do think that moth came from? Come on!"

The thought roused all six of them. Somewhere above them, the crack in the stone must reach a gap to a bigger place that could sustain life. Maybe they could escape into another cavern, or something! The sides of stone now were soft with soil. After they scrambled up through a final twist in the shaft, a faint twinkle of light appeared above them.

They shuffled as fast as they could, straining to pull themselves up, loosening clawfuls of earth as they went. Feathers ripped off of their necks and backs. Muck smeared their bodies. Dandelion reached up, and her talon unexpectedly tapped a hard ceiling. She thought she had reached the end of the crevice. Groping, she felt an edge.

"What is it?" said Cloud-wing.

"There's a cover," said Dandelion. She ran her talons over the ceiling again. It was made of stone, faintly moist and furry with moss, and flat compared to the crevice walls. Dandelion raised the Leasorn gem. "It looks unnatural," she said. "Cloud-wing, I think it can be pushed away."

The archaeopteryxes' cries were louder, echoing from both ends of the shaft as if they were everywhere, above them and below them at once.

"Go ahead. I'll brace you. Stand on me."

Dandelion gave the Leasorn gem to Cloud-wing to free her talons. The birds below them offered their support, and they all edged up as far as they could. Dandelion hesitated. One misstep, and they would all go tumbling down into the wings of the archaeopteryxes.

"Don't worry, just do it!" he cried.

Dandelion raised her talons and strained, stifling a scream when she felt Cloud-wing sliding down a little below her. She closed her eyes and pushed harder. They heard a grinding creak.

Pandey yelped. "The archaeopteryxes, they're coming nearer!"

Isobello, farthest down, took out his sling and started shooting pebbles blindly, rapidly down the shaft. Tightly packed, the archaeopteryxes howled below. "I still have enough pebbles," he said. "I think I can hold them off a few seconds."

"The cover moved," Dandelion whispered. "I see a crack." The four birds below repositioned themselves while Isobello continued to shoot.

"Your sword!" said Cloud-wing. "Use it, Dandelion."

Dandelion drew her weapon and carefully raised the steel blade. She wedged it into the crack as far as it would go. She leaned on the hilt.

The stone protested and shifted.

"Push!" They pressed close together. Dandelion summoned all her strength and shoved the stone aside.

They saw light. Dandelion used her sword to brace herself and climb out of the shaft. She turned, crouched, and helped Cloud-wing. Together they pulled up the rest of their companions. Dandelion stared at the black-and-white floor she was now standing on, recognizing the throne room in the Castle of Sky as eagle guards dashed in from all sides to see what the commotion was.

"Archaeopteryxes in our mountain!" Dandelion shouted, trying to slam the tile back over the crack they'd come from. She was too late. Kawaka barged out, flinging the slab of stone across the chamber at the guards. His recruits hurled themselves into the chamber, one after another.

Kawaka surveyed the scene. The Castle of Sky, in the heart of the golden eagles' stronghold! There was the empty throne waiting for him once he cleared the castle. *I will rule over both the Castle of Sky and the Castle of Earth,* he thought. "Charge!" he shouted to his soldiers. "Claim the castle for the empire!"

Dandelion lifted her sword as she squinted in the bright light streaming from the windows. A wave of dizziness hit her as if she'd flown too high. Too much, too long. The old archaeopteryx scars on her wings and back pulsed with burning pain.

No, she said to herself.

Boom, boom, boom. The sound reverberated, giving Dandelion strength and allowing her to focus. She looked up. A swarm of eaglets filled the room: Fleydur's students, the children of the court. There was Pudding, pounding furiously upon his drum to summon more help. And there was Olga, her ankle ribbons flying as she sent a kick into the behind of an archaeopteryx fighting with an eagle guard.

Cloud-wing shouted to Pudding, and they dashed into the antechamber where the Iron Nest gathered before coming to court. As Dandelion and the other Rockbottom students joined the few castle guards in the battle, the two reappeared with the voting stones of the Iron Nest. Within moments, the eaglets were armed with the big black cubes, hurling yeas and nays left and right upon the heads of the archaeopteryxes.

"Nay to archaeopteryxes!" cried Pudding.

"Yea for our homeland!" cried Cloud-wing.

Howling, archaeopteryxes clutched bruised eyes and cracked beaks as they and the eagles fought across the black-and-white checkered floor.

"Are you okay, Dandelion?" said Olga, appearing alongside her. "Where is your crown, and where are your acorns?"

Dandelion touched her collar, remembering how she

thought she would never have a use for them. And yet they had served their purpose as markers, as weapons, as bandage ties. . . .

Along the way, she had gathered something more. Friends who were alive. Love for her mountain. Hope for Fleydur.

Gripping her sword, Dandelion realized she didn't have to attend Rockbottom to be pounded to bits and be put together again. Her various past selves hovered in her mind, as if she was looking at her reflections in the Hall of Mirrors. She had been a peasant, a princess, and now, a warrior. She was not afraid to face an enemy alone anymore. She was her own army.

Kawaka cleaved left and right at his enemies, searching for the eagle with the gemstone. His furnace wounds goaded him like the sting of fire ants. He found Dandelion at last, by the bronze scales. Dandelion pointed her sword at Kawaka, the bird who had snuffed her sky-born candle and taken her parents from her.

"Eagles don't back down from a rough wind, but always dare to ride on it."

They locked eyes. "Do I know you?" he asked.

"You will know me now. I am Dandelion," she said. "You will not hurt me again, or hurt my home, Sword Mountain."

Kawaka raised his cutlass and lunged toward Dandelion. Dandelion twirled her sword, knocking the blow aside. In the opening that she'd made, she rushed closer and battered Kawaka across the cheek with her wings, and then spun out of range before the archaeopteryx could snap his beak on her feathers. They fought around and around the bronze eagle statue of justice, whose scales hung from its open wings.

Then Dandelion felt her sword wrenched from her grasp. When she flew down to retrieve it, Kawaka closed in. Her claws touched something else on the ground. She clutched it. A purple voting stone. She hurled it at Kawaka with all her might. Kawaka ducked; the stone struck the scales instead. Dandelion snatched up her sword again and rose. Looming behind Kawaka, the bronze eagle swayed, its scales creaking.

"Sword Mountain is mine," Kawaka shouted.

The scales slowly tipped forward, as if the bronze eagle was swooping—one edge of the base left the ground. Sensing something was amiss, Kawaka paused to look up, and in that very moment the scales crashed onto him with a thunderous noise.

The fighting ceased immediately.

The bronze eagle had not cracked; neither its wings nor its beak had broken from the impact. Rather, it lay very still, hunched forward as if brooding eggs, and Kawaka's claws, which poked out from under one of its scales, were unmoving.

Unnerved, the few remaining archaeopteryxes bolted toward a window, smashed the glass, and fled. Guards shot arrows after them.

The rest of the mourning train hurried inside. The king, in his death garments, teetered in the doorway. "Our kingdom was on the brink of death. Though famed for our sharpness of sight, we eagles were blind. We—of the strongest army, of the bravest fighters, of the highest peaks—we believed that Sword Mountain would never fall to forces from the outside. Yet it was nearly destroyed, hollowed and undermined by weaknesses and intrigue within."

Forlath's gaze fell on Dandelion and the Leasorn gem in her claws. "The gemstone has been found!" he exclaimed.

Dandelion, Cloud-wing, and the band of Rockbottom students explained their story. "It was Tranglarhad who stole the gemstone, and he was working together with the archaeopteryxes, beneath our mountain," Dandelion concluded.

"I don't believe it. How can our mountain have any such fault lines?" cried Sigrid. But the guards examined the floor beneath the throne and confirmed it.

"What fools you are. How could Fleydur have done anything to me?" said Morgan. "My sickness was not caused by him, but by a certain golden pill. I took it the morning of my birthday with my breakfast, as you remember, Sigrid. Where did you get that pill?"

"I believe it was a gift from somebird at court," said Sigrid. She winced at a sudden memory. "Tranglarhad," she said in a very small voice. Sigrid covered her face with a set of talons, upset by her own credulity and the owl's betrayal. She had been manipulated to administer the poison pill to the king!

"Your Majesty," said Dandelion to the king, "then may Fleydur be released?"

"Yes. Oh, my poor son!"

So the word traveled from one guard to another: "Open the dungeon. Free the prisoner. The king is alive and well!"

"Free Fleydur."

"Free Fleydur!"

Gemstone in claw, Dandelion flew, all the hundred joyous images of her rushing alongside her in the Hall of Mirrors. She spiraled down the staircase, toward the dungeon, and the birds in her way parted to let her rush by. As the dungeon gate creaked open, Dandelion held the purple gem up high, its glow so bright that she needed no torch to guide her.

"Fleydur! You're free. You've been proven innocent!" she cried. "And King Morgan is really alive." She showed him the gemstone. As the bars slid aside, Dandelion leaped into Fleydur's embrace.

"My brave, strong, bright flower," he said.

A song can be sung once but can be heard forever.
—FROM THE *OLD SCRIPTURE*

27

Excerpt From Songs And Records Of Fleydur

Whenever I sing this tale of the mountain, others ask me whether I had returned to be king. I never considered it, I tell them. "Why did you endure the persecution, then?" they want to know. To be honest, I longed for a sight of my old father, but I also felt a responsibility to change Sword Mountain. I wanted to bring a little joy and a little music to the cold summit.

And so, as time passes, and the long, black shadow of Sword Cliff sweeps in countless revolutions around the mountain, it is with pride and delight that I write that the school of my dreams has been established. As Forlath became king, my father and Sigrid moved to a cottage next to the castle. At last the Iron Nest gave me its approval to build a school at Double Pain Peak. The Vision School is, foremost, a place filled with happiness. It is a music conservatory, and by merging the Rockbottom Academy and the Castle of Sky seminary into it, it is also an institute of martial arts, sciences, and the philosophies. I believe that youngsters should discover who they are and explore what their talents are, rather than being forced to choose between becoming a musician, a warrior, or a scholar. Anybird with the motivation can attend the Vision School. I remember seeing all of the hopeful faces in the opening ceremony: Dandelion, Cloud-wing, and so many others from Sword Mountain, but also seagulls and parrots from far away.

All this might not have been possible without Dandelion. While I brought music to the summit, I believe Dandelion taught Sword Mountain something just as important. She showed that a valley orphan could make friends with anybird on the mountaintop. I shall sing of her story to the hatchlings and fledglings in every forest, desert, and sea: how a dandelion seed can thrive happily wherever it is blown.

Now, as music fills our mountains, I feel the silence in other places. The world beyond Sword Mountain needs me, too. When my old friend Winger the woodpecker scribe asked me if I would like to spread the *Old Scripture* with him, I knew it was time to put on my bard's garb again and bid good-bye to Sword Mountain. My father held my claws in his rough old talons and nodded. "Go, my son," he said. "With a new generation of birds like Dandelion, strong and joyous, the kingdom will be in good wings."

Farewell, Sword Mountain! I shall sing of you from the corners of the world.

Fleydur

Hope be with you as you rise.
—FROM THE *OLD SCRIPTURE*

RISING

Before the sun emerged to warm the crisp autumn sky, Dandelion and Cloud-wing stood on the summit of Sword Mountain.

The curved rooftop of the Vision School beckoned to them from the other end of the mountain range. Dandelion's backpack was ready; her sword was strapped at her side. Dandelion would have a new place to flourish, but she would never forget Sword Mountain. It was the place where she was hurt and healed, where she grew up and grew strong.

"I've made a sky lantern," Dandelion told Cloud-wing. She held a small bamboo cross in her claws, which was fitted inside a cylinder made of thin, waxed paper.

On the paper she had written:

Mother, Father,

I miss you. Don't worry, I am thriving.

Your Dandelion

In the middle of the flat cross she placed the sky-born candle from long ago. Dandelion had kept it with her always but never dared to light it, for she'd been afraid that it would burn away too quickly, leaving her with emptiness. She remembered clearly how it had lit up the faces of her mother and father. Now she was finally ready to light it again.

Dandelion lit the candle. As Cloud-wing steadied the bamboo frame, she held up the waxed paper balloon. Tears spilled from her eyes, but they were not just of sadness now.

The two eagles watched the paper globe billowing with warmth, slowly expanding, trembling with life.

"Let go," Dandelion whispered.

She and Cloud-wing stepped back. And the lantern

rose by itself, illuminating their faces, then rising gently over their heads.

"It's so beautiful, Dandelion," Cloud-wing said.

Over the mountaintop, in the wind, it sailed. It swayed gently in the silken breeze, circled around Sword Cliff and beyond. It was a miracle that a single small birthday candle could cast so much light and propel this vessel toward the faint stars in the black dome of sky, till it seemed a star itself.

Dandelion had no doubt now. *"To fly, there must be a special force inside you."* And she had given the candle her force.

As she flew toward the Vision School with Cloud-wing, she closed her eyes. In her mind she saw the little lantern, filled with hope and love, rising, rising, as night swept into day.

MAJOR CHARACTERS

Characters are golden eagles unless stated otherwise.

AMICUS—the secretary of the court.

BLAZE—a student at Rockbottom Academy.

BLITZ—a student at Rockbottom Academy.

CLOUD-WING—friend of Dandelion; four-acorn eaglet; son of the general of the Sword Mountain army.

DANDELION—a valley-born eaglet, brought to live on the mountaintop.

FLEYDUR—prince; elder son of Morgan, King of Skythunder; bard.

FORLATH—prince; younger son of Morgan, King of Skythunder; brother of Fleydur.

ISOBELLO—peregrine falcon; a student at Rockbottom Military Academy.

KAWAKA—archaeopteryx; former head knight of the archaeopteryx empire; ally of Tranglarhad.

MORGAN—King of Skythunder, whose castle is on Sword Mountain; leader of the Skythunder tribe of eagles; husband of Sigrid; father of Fleydur and Forlath.

OLGA—half-acorn eaglet.

PANDEY—osprey; a student at Rockbottom Academy.

POULDINGTON—four-acorn eaglet; son of the treasurer of Sword Mountain; nicknamed Pudding.

SIGRID—Queen of Skythunder; second wife of Morgan; mother of Forlath; stepmother of Fleydur.

SIMPLICIO—onetime tutor of the castle children; member of the Iron Nest.

TRANGLARHAD—eagle owl; High Owl of Optical Theories (H.O.O.T.), owner of the Knautyorsbut Mine under Sword Mountain; second tutor of the court children; ally of Kawaka.

URI—valet to Fleydur.

Acknowledgments

My deep thanks go to Ms. Phoebe Yeh, editorial director at HarperCollins Children's Books. It is she who has helped me all the way. Her careful eye, kind guidance, and unwavering belief in the Swordbird series have given me confidence to experiment and strive further.

I would like to thank other people at HarperCollins for their continuing support in all sorts of ways: Ms. Susan Katz, president of HarperCollins Children's Books; Ms. Kate Jackson, senior vice president of HarperCollins

Children's Books; Ms. Jean McGinley, subsidiary rights director; Ms. Jessica MacLeish; and the rest of the Harper team. Thanks also to Mr. Mark Zug for his beautiful cover art.

Special thanks are given to Ms. Oprah Winfrey for featuring me and the Swordbird series on her show; to Ms. Leah Wilson, editor, for inviting me to write an essay about animal fantasy for the anthology *Secrets of the Dragon Riders*; and to Mr. Wu Xiqing, president of the Vast Plain Publishing House in Taiwan, for his enthusiasm in publishing the traditional Chinese version of the Swordbird series.

My IB program teachers are all my Fleydurs and deserve many thanks. Their marvelous teaching gave me lots of inspiration for writing *Sword Mountain*. And, as always, I would like to thank Mrs. Diane Goodwin, one of my earliest teachers, whose care has been unwavering.

I am profoundly grateful to my grandparents, parents, relatives, and friends for their wholehearted support, which has never failed to fill me with the glow of a hundred candles.

Of course, I want to thank my birds as well—they are the original dancers of the schwa-schwa. In the midst of my writing, Ever-sky, my blue lovebird, laid six eggs, and the first baby lovebird hatched the day I finished my first draft.

Finally, thank you, my readers. Your curiosity and anticipation always propel me on.